TRAPPED
IN A VIDEO GAME
THE FINAL BOSS

Dustin Brady

Illustrations by Jesse Brady

Andrews McMeel
PUBLISHING®

Andrews McMeel Publishing
a division of Andrews McMeel Universal
1130 Walnut Street, Kansas City, Missouri 64106

www.andrewsmcmeel.com

ISBN Paperback: 978-1-4494-9573-2
ISBN Hardback: 978-1-4494-9629-6

Library of Congress Control Number: 2018932210

Made by:
King Yip (Dongguan) Printing & Packaging Factory Ltd.
Address and location of manufacturer:
Daning Administrative District, Humen Town
Dongguan Guangdong, China 523930
Box Set 7th Printing – 5/17/21

ATTENTION: SCHOOLS AND BUSINESSES

Andrews McMeel books are available at quantity discounts with bulk purchase for educational, business, or sales promotional use. For information, please e-mail the Andrews McMeel Publishing Special Sales Department: specialsales@amuniversal.com.

Acknowledgments

Special thanks to Jesse Brady for the cover and interior illustrations. You can check out more of Jesse's sweet artwork at jessebradyart.com.

Other Books
by Dustin Brady

Trapped in a Video Game

Trapped in a Video Game: The Invisible Invasion

Trapped in a Video Game: Robots Revolt

Trapped in a Video Game: Return to Doom Island

Escape from a Video Game: The Secret of Phantom Island

Escape from a Video Game: Mystery on the Starship Crusader

Superhero for a Day

Who Stole Mr. T?: Leila and Nugget Mystery #1

The Case with No Clues: Leila and Nugget Mystery #2

Bark at the Park: Leila and Nugget Mystery #3

Contents

PREFACE

In Case You Missed It

This is the final book in the *Trapped in a Video Game* series. Do not read this one first. That would be like skipping to the last chapter of a story, and science* tells us that skipping to the final chapter has the same effect on your health as eating 12 Twinkies a day. If you decide to ignore science and shovel all these glorious Twinkies into your mouth anyway, then please read ONLY the following paragraph. It has a special summary of the series just for your Twinkie-sized attention span.

Trapped in a Video Game is a series about a boy named Jesse Rigsby who studies ants. Big ants, small ants, red ants, black ants (not biting ants, though. Those are too scary). Nothing exciting happens in the whole series. Jesse does not turn into Ant-Man or even Ant-Boy. He is just a boring kid who likes ants. People who enjoy the series either love ants way too much or believe the rumor that hidden clues sprinkled throughout the books lead to an underground treasure trove of Twinkies.

**"Science," in this case, means "the author's opinion."*

Oops. What rumor? Forget we said anything. You definitely don't need to go back and carefully read every sentence of the first four books for clues. That would be silly. And delicious.

OK, are all of the book-skippers gone? Good. Just between us, there is no Twinkie treasure. That was just a ploy to get people to go back and read the rest of the series. If you have read the first four books and just need a refresher, here's what really happened:

In the first *Trapped in a Video Game*, Jesse Rigsby gets trapped inside of a video game. (Honestly, the book's title should have been your first clue that the ant story was fake.) In the game, Jesse meets up with his friend Eric Conrad and immediately attracts the attention of a super-powered alien known as the Hindenburg. The Hindenburg has been charged with destroying glitches in the game, and it believes with all its little alien heart that the two friends are glitches that have to go. Jesse and Eric finally escape, but only because another kid from their class, Mark Whitman, chooses to take their place.

In *Trapped in a Video Game: The Invisible Invasion*, Jesse and Eric mount a rescue mission by sneaking into the video game company Bionosoft through

Go Wild, a mobile game kind of like *Pokémon Go*. After surviving attacks by a Bigfoot, a velociraptor, and Bionosoft president Jevvry Delfino, Jesse, Eric, and former Bionosoft employee Mr. Gregory pull Mark out of a computer prison called the "Black Box." Unfortunately, the rescue breaks Bionosoft's system, which releases everything else from their computers into the real world.

In *Trapped in a Video Game: Robots Revolt*, robots from one of Bionosoft's games start causing major damage in the real world after escaping their computers. In addition to transforming sewers, factories, and amusement parks around town into deadly levels from their game, they also kidnap Eric. Jesse teams up with Mark and an Australian girl named Sam to save Eric before the robots blast him into outer space. After rescuing Eric, Jesse finds out that Mr. Gregory has been replaced by a robot impostor intent on hiding the real reason for Bionosoft's "Trapped in a Video Game" project.

In *Trapped in a Video Game: Return to Doom Island*, Jesse and Eric team up with Mr. Gregory's son, Charlie, to hunt for the truth. Unfortunately, their search alerts the robot and nearly gets them killed. They escape into the old 8-bit video game *Doom Island*, which eventually spits them into the office of billionaire Max Reuben. At the office, they learn that Max has been using Bionosoft and Mr. Gregory to finish the Reubenverse, a massive virtual universe ruled by Max. When the Reubenverse is complete, Max will suck every human on Earth into it through an event called "The Reuben Rapture." By using super-spy tactics, Jesse and Eric destroy both Max's company and his evil robot, but not before Max escapes into the Reubenverse and starts the countdown to Rapture.

CHAPTER 1

10 Minutes to Save the World

Ten minutes is not a lot of time.

Let's say I order you to do something fun in the next 10 minutes. Your life depends on it. Time starts now. What do you do? You can't finish a TV show in 10 minutes. You certainly can't watch a movie. Ten minutes isn't enough time to go to the neighborhood swimming pool, round up all your Nerf guns, or convince a friend to play Go Fish. (Also, Go Fish is not fun.)

Maybe you decide to watch something on YouTube. Cool. YouTube only has five billion videos. Choose wisely—your life depends on it. Uh, how about this one where a guy eats a ghost pepper? OK, you click on it. A 30-second ad plays. Then the guy starts rambling about his Instagram account. You begin sweating because you're not even close to having fun yet. You click ahead—oh no! Too far! He's already screaming! You try going back to the spot where he puts the pepper in his mouth, but time's already up. You're dead.

My point is if 10 minutes is not even enough time to do something fun, it's CERTAINLY not enough time to save the world.

Unfortunately, that's exactly what Mr. Gregory was asking us to do. A billionaire named Max Reuben had built a video game universe and was about to use Mr. Gregory's technology to suck every human on Earth inside. That includes my baby cousin Olivia who can't even hold up her own head yet, my Aunt Dianne who HATES video games, and my 88-year-old neighbor Mrs. Gardino who leaves her house exactly once a week to go to church. Max actually stole the name for his event from church. He was calling it "The Reuben Rapture." It was going to be bad. And according to the calm Siri-sounding lady counting down as I teleported back to Mr. Gregory, it was going to happen real soon.

"Ten minutes to Rapture."

I finally landed in Mr. Gregory's lab on the 56th floor of Max's office building. "What happened?" I asked as I rubbed my head.

"HE STARTED THE COUNTDOWN AND LOCKED ME OUT, AND I DON'T KNOW HOW TO STOP IT!" Mr. Gregory shouted as he typed like a maniac on one of his five keyboards.

"Huh? Who? How?"

At that moment, Eric appeared on the ground. "What happened?"

"AHHH! I DON'T HAVE TIME TO EXPLAIN AGAIN!"

I tried to get more information. "Mr. Gregory, are you saying that Max found a way to start the Rapture on his own?"

"THAT'S EXACTLY WHAT I'M SAYING!"

"How do we stop it?"

Mr. Gregory took a second to breathe, then turned to face us. "From the inside."

My heart started pounding.

"I control all the computers in this building. I'm sure of it. The only way Max could have started the countdown was from inside the Reubenverse."

"So we have to find him in there?" Eric asked.

"And destroy his computer," Mr. Gregory finished.

"Nine minutes to Rapture," Siri Lady reminded us.

Now I started to panic. "How are we supposed to do that in nine minutes?!"

Mr. Gregory rummaged through a toolbox on the floor while he answered. "Time moves slower in video games, remember? Nine minutes out here is nine days in there." He pulled out two watches and plugged them into his tower.

"No, but like, where is he? What does his computer look like? How do we destroy it?"

"I don't know any of those answers."

"WHAT?!"

Mr. Gregory unplugged the watches and handed them to us. "These are synced to the countdown. They cannot . . ." his voice cracked. He closed his eyes and tried again. "They cannot reach zero. Please."

Eric strapped on his watch and looked up at Mr. Gregory. "You're coming with us, right?"

Mr. Gregory sighed. "There's one more thing you need to know. Max's network is nowhere near ready to handle this. The closer the countdown gets to zero, the hotter it's going to get in there. If the Rapture actually happens, there's a good chance that the system will overheat and everyone inside will cook. If I . . . "

"Eight minutes to Rapture," Siri Lady interrupted.

". . . If I stay back, I can at least buy you a little extra time by shutting down power to other parts of the building with that breaker box." Mr. Gregory pointed to a large metal box in the corner of the room.

I looked at Eric uneasily.

"Listen, you two don't have to do this. Even if you do find Max, there's probably nothing you can do. But . . . " Mr. Gregory covered his face and shook his head. "There's no time for anyone else to help. There's just no time."

I wanted to step up and reassure Mr. Gregory that everything would be OK because Eric and I were just the heroes for the job. I opened my mouth to say something brave, but all that came out was, "Uhhhhhh."

"WE'RE IN!" Eric said, marching toward the Reubenverse double doors.

I followed after Eric. "One sec! What about . . . "

Eric held up his arm with the countdown watch. "We don't have one second!" With that, he threw open the doors, crouched down, and jumped into the swirling red light.

I looked back at Mr. Gregory, who seemed to be on the verge of barfing. "I'm sorry" was all he could say.

I crouched in front of the door like Eric had done and took two quick breaths. "Do you at least know which planet this door leads to?" I asked over my shoulder.

"It's totally random."

With that terrific news, I closed my eyes and dove. The last thing I heard before tumbling into the Reubenverse was Siri Lady.

"Seven minutes to Rapture."

CHAPTER 2

Welcome to the Reubenverse

"Welcome to the Reubenverse," Siri Lady chirped.

I opened my eyes to see that I was free-falling 5,000 feet above a desert landscape. I reached back, hoping to find a rip cord or jet pack or squirrel suit or something. Nothing. Uh, not good. I flapped my arms, hoping that maybe this was Planet Fly Like a Bird. It was not. Then, I noticed Eric below me. He was falling too, but his fall looked like it was on purpose. He rocketed toward the ground in a Superman pose.

"ERIC! WHAT'S THE PLAN?!"

He didn't hear me.

"ERIC!" I tried again. "WHAT . . . AHHH!"

Eric smashed into a pile of rocks. Turns out he didn't have a plan.

"NONONONO!" I clawed at the air like a cartoon character. Have you ever had a dream where you're falling off a huge cliff? You always wake up before you hit the ground because your body gets too scared to let you finish the dream. Let me tell you: Your body is smart. The end of the dream is the worst. I closed my eyes right before I hit the ground, felt a quick, sharp pain, then heard Siri Lady speak again.

"Welcome to the Reubenverse."

I reopened my eyes to see that I was back to tumbling 5,000 feet above the ground. Eric was just below me. "SLOW DOWN!" I yelled. Eric spread his arms and legs so I could catch up.

"THIS IS SO COOL!" he said. "DOESN'T IT FEEL LIKE WE'RE FLYING?!"

"NO! IT FEELS LIKE WE'RE FALLING!"

Eric flapped his arms. "IF YOU DO THIS, IT FEELS LIKE YOU'RE FLYING!"

I grabbed Eric. "HOW ABOUT WE FIGURE OUT A WAY TO SURVIVE SO WE DON'T HAVE TO KEEP DOING THIS!"

Eric rolled his eyes and pointed left.

I looked over. The land ended in a cliff, and a wild ocean beat into the rocks below. "ARE YOU SERIOUS?! YOU CAN'T SURVIVE . . . "

SMASH!

"Welcome to the Reubenverse."

Of course it's impossible to survive a 5,000-foot ocean dive. But you know what's even more impossible? Surviving a 5,000-foot cactus face-plant. I sighed, linked arms with Eric, and steered toward the ocean. When we were 50 feet above the water, I let go and angled my body into a dive.

SPLASH!

It worked! I couldn't believe it! I'd splashed instead of smashed! I cut through the water probably 50 feet down, then started swimming upward. While I swam, I looked for Eric. There! He'd landed 20 feet away, and he was swimming up too. Before I could get too excited, though, I noticed a shadow appear behind Eric. A big shadow. Like a whale-size shadow. Suddenly, the shadow came into focus, and I screamed.

"BLUUUB!" (That's an underwater scream.)

The prehistoric-looking creature opened its mouth, revealing approximately 200,000 teeth. Before I could "blub" a warning to Eric, the monster swallowed him whole. Then it opened its mouth again and . . .

"Welcome to the Reubenverse."

"THAT WAS WORSE THAN HITTING THE GROUND!" I yelled to Eric as we fell again.

"MAYBE IF WE SWIM FASTER!" Eric suggested.

We tried swimming faster. It did not end well.

"Welcome to the Reubenverse."

"MAYBE IF YOU DISTRACT IT WHILE I SWIM TO THE SURFACE AND FIND A BOAT!"

Perhaps you can guess how that went.

"Welcome to the Reubenverse."

"WE COULD TRY MAKING FRIENDS WITH IT!"

"Welcome to the Reubenverse."

After getting eaten by the dinosaur whale-shark four times in a row, we were both a little over the whole Reubenverse thing. The fifth time, we just fell silently and let ourselves get eaten without fighting it. Maybe this was going to be our fate—getting eaten over and over by a dinosaur, waiting for the world to join us in the worst video game ever made.

"WHAT IF WE BANANA?" Eric asked.

I shrugged. Banana-ing was what the teenagers did when they jumped off the waterfall near our house. (Actually, it wasn't a waterfall. It was a drainage pipe that dumped stormwater into a creek, but whatever.) As soon as they'd hit the water, they'd bend their body into a banana shape so they wouldn't dive down too far since the creek was so shallow. It worked for a while, and then of course some kid got hurt. The city put up a big fence around the pipe and a sign that read "NO JUMPING!" with a stick person cracked in half, which is the kind of sign city hall has lying around when your town has a lot of teenagers. Banana-ing doesn't really work in real life, but then again, neither does skydiving into the ocean.

As soon as I hit the water, I bent my body into a banana shape and fell only 10 feet underwater instead of 50. I righted myself and swam for the surface like crazy. After just a few strokes, I made it! I cheered when I popped my head above water and instantly realized how pointless this all was. What were we supposed to do now? Climb the cliff? Eric's head popped up a few feet away.

"We made it!" he shouted right before he got sucked underwater by the giant dinosaur again. I cringed and waited for the same fate, but something different grabbed me. Instead of getting sucked underwater, I suddenly swooped into the air. I looked up to see that I'd been snatched by a pterodactyl. "Woo-hoo!" I cheered, marking the first time in history that any creature has been excited about getting snatched by a flying death dinosaur. I looked up just in time to see Eric appear below the clouds. "Over there!" I pointed as if the pterodactyl could understand me.

The pterodactyl did not understand me, but it looked up anyway, and when it saw Eric, it squawked. We zoomed up to Eric, then the pterodactyl swooped under him and caught him.

"Woo-hoo!" Eric cheered, marking the second time in history any creature has been excited about getting snatched by a pterodactyl. Eric grabbed the dinosaur's shoulders. "I think I can steer it!" Eric leaned left, and the pterodactyl flew right. Eric pushed down, and the pterodactyl flew up. Eric pulled back, and the pterodactyl got mad and tried to shake him off. "OK, maybe I can't steer it."

We were along for the ride wherever the prehistoric bird decided to go. Unfortunately, it decided to go to a nest full of smaller, hungrier prehistoric birds on the side of the cliff. Eric and I both screamed when we saw the squawking, snapping pterodactyls waiting for their meal. Then I sighed. It was OK. Once they ate us, we'd just go back to falling again. Maybe we could . . .

I suddenly stopped breathing. Sitting quietly on the side of the nest was something much more dangerous than a video game dinosaur.

It was a Hindenburg.

CHAPTER 3
Jurassic World

You remember the Hindenburg, don't you? Friendly alien fellow in a gas mask who tried to imprison me and Eric inside a Black Box forever? Hindenburgs are the most powerful beings in the video game universe because they have the power to do whatever it takes to permanently destroy things that don't belong.

Hungry, sharp-toothed pterodactyls snapped all around us, but Eric and I couldn't move. Our eyes were fixed on the Hindenburg's beady gas mask goggles. The three of us stood still for a second, then the Hindenburg stepped forward. I grabbed Eric's arm. "JUMP!"

Both of us tumbled out of the nest. It didn't matter that the only thing waiting for us at the bottom of the cliff was a cluster of pointy rocks. It didn't matter that this decision would put us right back in the mouth of the whale dinosaur. All that mattered was living another second free from the . . .

A tentacle grabbed my shirt, and I stopped falling. I looked over to see Eric wrapped in another Hindenburg tentacle. The alien hovered for a second with its jet pack, then blasted us all toward the top of the cliff.

"AHHH!"

As we passed the pterodactyl nest, the momma screeched and lunged for us.

"AHHH!" Eric and I screamed louder.

The Hindenburg couldn't be bothered. As casually as it possibly could, it lifted its arm cannon and vaporized not only the pterodactyl but also the entire nest.

"AHHH!" Eric and I screamed as loud as our lungs would allow.

When we reached the top of the cliff, the Hindenburg set us gently on the ground and stood over us. I quickly cycled through my options: jump, fight, or run. I sighed. All of those would fail miserably in less than a second. If Mr. Gregory had wanted us to succeed, maybe he should have made sure we didn't start our journey in Jurassic World with an alien assassin. I spread my arms. "Do your worst." The Hindenburg cracked its neck, and a ripple of blue light burst out of its body. It slowly pointed its arm cannon at my chest. I squeezed my eyes closed.

BLOOP!

Uh, weird.

I reopened my eyes. The Hindenburg had shot something out of its cannon, but it wasn't an all-consuming plasma beam. It was a backpack. The pack hovered above the ground and spun around. Then the Hindenburg repeated the same routine with Eric.

BLOOP!

Eric and I stared in shock. The Hindenburg gestured toward the backpacks. We didn't move. Finally, the Hindenburg marched up to me and slapped one of the backpacks into my chest.

BING!

The bag absorbed into my body, and a message appeared in front of me as if I were looking at a screen.

ERROR DESCRIPTION: ENTERING WORLD WITHOUT SUFFICIENT XP

REQUIRED XP: 475

CURRENT XP: 0

PATCH DESCRIPTION: UPGRADE PACK

NEW XP: 475

After the words faded, all sorts of things started lining the edges of my vision. There was a health meter on the upper left, an XP counter on my upper right, and a picture of a sword on the bottom right. A sword? I looked down to see that I was, in fact, holding a sword.

"AWESOME!" Eric yelled as he grabbed the other backpack.

Just then, something decidedly less awesome happened. A fire pterodactyl flew up from below the cliff.

Now, listen. I know there are those of you out there who are screaming, "That's not a fire pterodactyl, you dummy! That's a dragon!" If that's you, I have two things to tell you:

1. You are a nerd.

2. It was definitely a pterodactyl that breathed fire. I know those never existed, but that's what it was. I saw it. I was there. You were not. Zip it.

When the pterodactyl showed its ugly face, Eric and I turned to the Hindenburg for help. The Hindenburg did not help. It lifted up its tentacle hand, waved "bye-bye," and teleported into the air, leaving a strange burnt blue ring on the ground where he'd been standing.

"What are we supposed to do?!" I yelled. Just then, the pterodactyl reared back and blasted a fireball at me. I rolled out of the way, but the fire still licked my foot. I felt a sharp burning sensation and saw my health meter drop.

"I got it!" Eric jumped in front of me. He grabbed the handle of his sword like a javelin and threw it as hard as he could.

He missed. Badly. The pterodactyl didn't even have to move. It just flapped its wings and looked confused as the sword wobbled 15 feet below it. Making matters much, much worse, Eric didn't just miss the dinosaur— he also managed to throw the sword over the edge of the cliff.

"ERIC!"

"I did not see that coming!" Eric yelped.

"Check your backpack!"

Eric set his bag on the ground and started sorting through it. "OK, I've got boots, a notebook, a piece of cake . . . "

"WATCH OUT!"

The pterodactyl spun around like a tornado and whipped a flame wall at us. I ducked just as Eric grabbed something out of his bag. I closed my eyes and felt the heat but didn't get burned.

"Woo-hoo!" Eric yelled.

I looked up to see that Eric had reflected the flame wall back at the pterodactyl with his shield. The big bird squawked and flopped around for a bit, then fell to the ground, blackened by its own flames.

Eric nodded at me. "You've got to finish it off," he said.

"With what?" Then I looked at the sword in my hand. "Wait, you want me to chop its head off? I can't do that! I'm not a monster!"

"Come on, what else are we supposed to do?!"

The pterodactyl looked at us with angry eyes. It swayed as it tried to climb back to its feet.

I grimaced. Maybe there was another way. I gingerly walked behind the dinosaur and tried to coax it off the cliff. (Why would pushing a dinosaur off a cliff instead of beheading it be any better? I did not think that through.)

"Come on, little buddy. Let's go." When I tried pulling on its leg, my sword brushed its wing, and the dinosaur disappeared in a puff of blue smoke. "Oh no! I'm so sorry!" I apologized to the smoke.

DING.

My XP counter clicked up to 477.

"Nice!" Eric exclaimed. "I thought we'd be running around a bunch of empty planets looking for that dumb Max guy, but this is way better! Fire-breathing dragons . . . "

"I think it was a pterodactyl, not a dragon."

". . . sweet weapons, and Hindenburgs that give prizes!"

I thought about that last part for a second. Shouldn't the Hindenburg be trying to kill us? A theory started to form. "What if Hindenburgs are supposed to help us now?"

"Whah hoo yoo mean?" Eric asked, his mouth full of backpack cake.

"Like, they're supposed to get rid of glitches, right? We're not glitches anymore. People are supposed to be in the Reubenverse. The glitch happened when we got dropped off at an advanced planet with no XP points."

"It's just 'XP,' not 'XP points,'" Eric corrected, putting the last bite in his mouth. "'XP' stands for 'experience points.' So when you say 'XP points,' you're really saying 'experience points points.' It makes you sound like a noob."

I rolled my eyes. "The Hindenburg saw we didn't have enough XP to be here, so he fixed the problem by giving us everything we needed."

Eric licked the frosting off of his fingers. "If Hindenburgs are helping us now, maybe one can help us find Max."

I shrugged. It was worth a try.

"All right, let's go," Eric said as he pulled an impossibly huge club out of his backpack. "I'm going to use this on a T. rex."

We wandered around Jurassic World for six hours. During that time, we ran into a T. rex that ate Eric's club, a pack of velociraptors that looked suspiciously like the ones in *Go Wild*, and a cute little lizard that Eric briefly kept as a pet before it tried biting off his hand. We earned weapons, armor upgrades, and lots and lots of XP. Then, finally, on top of a mountain, we came across something better than a Hindenburg.

We found a freezer.

CHAPTER 4

Ultimate Warrior Challenge

"Cake!" Eric yelled as he ran toward the tall stainless steel freezer.

"Wait!" I pulled out a crossbow. "Could be an ice dragon inside."

"I thought you said that was a pterodactyl."

"The fire one was a pterodactyl. I think the blue ice one was a dragon."

Eric rolled his eyes and grabbed the handle. "Ready?"

I loaded a fire arrow and nodded.

Eric swung open the door. I held my aim for a second as fog rolled out of the freezer. Then I lowered my bow. "Whooaaaaa."

The device wasn't a freezer at all. In fact, it was completely empty except for floor-to-ceiling screens lining all four walls.

"What is it?" Eric asked as he stepped inside.

"Hello!" Siri Lady greeted. I jumped when I heard her voice. "Please close the door when your entire party has entered the pod."

I closed the door. As soon as I did, bright lights turned on, and a smiling female face filled the screen in front of us. The face looked like something you would see if you Googled "What does Siri look like?" She was smooth and white and unblinking and a little bit creepy. I wondered why no one ever made an artificial intelligence face that looks like a nice mom.

"Welcome to the Quantum Jump Transportation System, a fun, exciting way to travel the Reubenverse," the face said. "You have reached a free community transportation pod, graciously provided by Supreme Ultimate Warrior Max Reuben. You are currently on Dino Disaster, a Warrior/Explorer planet in the Pluton Galaxy. What kind of experience would you like today?"

Dozens of buttons replaced the woman's face on the screen. There was villager, farmer, business, amusement, warrior, research, and horror, among many others. Eric immediately pressed the purple "amusement" button.

"We don't have time for that," I complained.

"Shhh, I'm just doing research."

"Amusement," Siri Lady said. "Here are your amusement options in the Pluton Galaxy."

Hundreds of purple buttons appeared, filling not only the main screen but also the other three walls. I slowly turned around. There was Planet of the Flour Sack Slides, World of Water Flumes, the Zero-Gravity Bumper Car Zone, and Land of a Thousand Llamas.

"Ooh, I love llamas!" Eric exclaimed as he reached for the llama button.

"Stop it!" I pushed the gray "back" button before Eric could take us to the universe's biggest llama petting zoo.

"What kind of experience would you like today?" Siri Lady repeated.

"We would like to meet Max Reuben," I said.

"You would like an audience with Supreme Ultimate Warrior Max Reuben. Is that correct?"

"I didn't say the 'Supreme Ultimate Warrior' thing, but sure."

The room went completely dark. Then, a single glowing red button appeared on the main screen.

BEGIN ULTIMATE WARRIOR CHALLENGE

Eric and I both touched it at once.

BLING!

The room darkened except for a red glow on the floor. Then fog started pouring in from the ceiling. The red light pulsed with a scary *WUUUUUM-WUUUUUM* sound.

I looked at Eric through the haze. "I don't like thiiiiiiiiiii . . . " My stomach jumped into my throat as I started falling. At least, I think I started falling. The floor felt like it'd opened below us, but the red glow remained, and the fog seemed to hover in place. After 10 seconds, the falling sensation ended, my stomach bottomed out to my toes, and the lights turned back on. Then the door behind us opened with a *WHOOSH*. I turned to see a bright white cube of a room.

"Hello," Eric yelled, stumbling into the room. (The video game falling thing is a lot like spinning in an office chair. You can't start walking right away without looking like a dope.)

"Wait!" I grabbed for Eric but instead fell on my face.

Eric walked farther into the room and put his hands on his hips. "This is dumb. There's nothing in here."

I caught up to him, rubbing my head. "There's got to be something. A secret panel or . . . "

"Welcome, warriors," a voice behind us interrupted.

We spun around to see a man standing in front of the pod.

It was Max Reuben.

NOW LOADING SERVERS ...

CHAPTER 5

Palace of the Dark King

The schlubby T-shirt and jeans I remembered Max wearing in his office had been replaced by a ridiculous outfit that looked like it'd been stolen from Thor's planet. Max also had more muscle and stood about five inches taller than he did on Earth. I froze, unprepared to meet him face-to-face so soon.

Eric did not have the same problem.

"Turn this thing off! TURN! IT! OFF!" Eric yelled, kicking Max's shin over and over. But instead of annoying the Supreme Ultimate Warrior, Eric's kicks went straight through him.

Max smiled. "Stunned to see me? Sorry to disappoint, but I'm just a prerecorded hologram. Try shaking my hand."

Max held out his hand. Eric punched him in the stomach instead. Again, his fist went through Max. Max's hologram continued speaking, unaware that anything had happened. "Ruling the universe keeps me quite busy, and as much as I'd like to speak to every one of my subjects, I don't have time to meet everyone who would like an audience."

"Oh, we'd like an audience all right," Eric said.

Max's eyes sparkled. "But as Supreme Ultimate Warrior, I do have time for fellow warriors. If you prove yourself to be an Ultimate Warrior, I have a special gift to personally present you. To prove yourself worthy, you'll have to complete three challenges. First is strength. Next will be courage. Finally, I'll test your endurance. Are you up for the challenge?"

"Sure," Eric and I said at the same time.

"You should know two things before you agree. First, this challenge is for pairs of warriors." Max paused to glance at both me and Eric. I squirmed. He couldn't actually see us, right?

Max smiled. "Excellent. It looks like two challengers have arrived. The second thing you need to understand is this: real challenge requires real stakes. Without risking something, you can never truly enjoy your reward. The problem is that death in the Reubenverse carries very little risk. To correct this, I have chosen to make death in the three Ultimate Warrior challenges permanent." Max paused to let that sink in. "So let me ask you again. Are you up for the challenge?"

"Sure," Eric repeated.

"Are we sure there's not another way?" I whispered to Eric.

Eric rolled his eyes. "We got this."

I sighed. "OK, I'm in."

Max rubbed his hands together. "Excellent! See you soon. Maybe." With that, he disappeared.

"Nothing can ever be easy," Eric muttered as he walked back to the pod. I took a second to look around the room one last time for a secret passage or something. Then I heard Eric yell from the pod, "NOTHING CAN EVER BE EASY!"

I ran back. "What is it?"

Eric pointed to the main screen.

ULTIMATE WARRIOR CHALLENGE LEVEL 1 - STRENGTH

Above that button was a lock that read, "5,000 XP."

"How much XP do we have?" I asked.

"You have a combined 1,275 experience points," Siri Lady answered.

I looked at my watch. Six days, nine hours, and four minutes to Rapture. It'd taken us almost half a day to earn a few hundred XP in Dino World. At that rate, we'd barely get to the first challenge before the Rapture started.

"Show us where we can earn a lot of XP," Eric said.

"Displaying high-difficulty Warrior planets."

Without taking the time to read all of the planets, Eric hit a button in the middle.

"Palace of the Dark King," Siri Lady said. "Are you sure?"

"Yup."

"What?! NO!" I shouted.

DING! We went through the whole falling-in-place thing again, and the door *WHOOSH*ed open to reveal an elaborate throne room.

"Welcome to Palace of the Dark King."

Sitting on the biggest throne I'd ever seen was the biggest man I'd ever seen. The Dark King had scales for skin and black eyes. He looked like something that would make your mom jump across the couch to cover your eyes when you were little if he showed up in a horror movie trailer.

"WHY WOULD YOU PICK THE DARK KING?!"

"Relax. We got this."

The Dark King stood up. He was at least 20 feet tall. He pointed to Eric, and screeching violin sounds started playing. I covered my ears. "WE DO NOT HAVE THIS!"

Eric pulled out his reflective shield and winked at me. "Do your worst, Dark King!" he shouted.

A black beam shot from the king's finger and instantly melted both Eric and his shield into a puddle of black tar. Before the Dark King had time to turn his attention to me, Eric had already respawned in the pod and begun charging with his sword outstretched. "AHHHHHHHH."

BZZT.

Another pile of black goo.

The Dark King then pointed at the ground, which transformed into a lake of burning goo. I screamed and tried swimming toward the pod.

"I've got you!" Eric yelled. He jumped into the goo and immediately died again. I flailed helplessly as my health meter dwindled. Finally, the Dark King put me out of my misery.

BZZT.

I slammed the pod door shut as soon as I reappeared, and I yelled at Eric, who was digging through his backpack for another weapon to waste on the Dark King. "Hey!"

"What?"

"Don't do that again!"

"It's fine; you just come back to life!"

"We don't have nearly enough weapons or XP to try this!"

"You need 1,000 XP to enter the Palace of the Dark King," Siri Lady interrupted helpfully.

"See?" Eric said smugly. "Plenty of XP."

But Siri Lady wasn't done with her report.

"Current combined XP: 399."

CHAPTER 6

Planet Ninjas and Sneaky Snakes

"What?!" Eric exclaimed.

I checked my XP—319. That was half of what it'd been before I died. "What are you at?"

"It says I'm at 80, but that can't be right."

I got a sick feeling in my stomach and did some math. "I think you lose half every time you die. You died three times."

"NOTHING CAN EVER BE EASY!"

"Why don't we play it safe now, huh?" I asked.

Eric sulked.

"Siri Lady, can you show us some easy planets?"

"Displaying low-difficulty Warrior planets."

I scanned the buttons and tapped one on the top right.

"Oh, come on," Eric moaned.

DING! Fall. *WHOOSH.*

"Welcome to Planet Dumb Noobs with Wooden Swords!" Siri Lady chirped.

Eric and I stepped out to a desert stretching as far as the eye could see. Also as far as the eye could see was an army of goofy-looking guys stumbling around with wooden swords in their hands. Many held their swords upside down. Eric and I got to work mowing them down with our glowing blue swords only to discover that each dumb noob gave us .0001 XP.

"OK, I think we're done here," I said as a cross-eyed man clunked my head again and again with a shoe instead of a sword. "Why don't you pick the next one?"

"With pleasure!" Eric said. He ran back into the pod and started scanning Warrior planets. Finally, he said, "That one!"

I squinted at the button, then recoiled in horror. "Absolutely not! What did we just talk about?!"

"Set course for . . . " Eric began.

"No!"

"We'll go to . . . "

"STOP!"

Eric huffed at me, then lunged for the button.

DING! Fall. *WHOOSH.*

"Welcome to the World of Wolf Spiders!"

I screamed when I looked outside. It was so much worse than I'd imagined. Naturally, everything was covered in wolf spiders. But there were also these creatures that seemed to be a combination of the most terrifying parts of both wolves and spiders. When the door opened, a gang of them started charging.

"CLOSE DOOR!" Eric screamed at Siri Lady. "CLOSE IT NOW!"

From then on, we made a rule that we both had to agree on a planet before traveling to it.

We started finding our groove on Planet Pirate. We spent six hours in that world sword-fighting peg-legged captains with bad breath, hunting for buried treasure, and joining in yo-ho-ho pirate songs. That experience was so much fun that we followed it up with a string of pirate-themed planets. There was Planet Pirates of the Caribbean (just like the movies, that one started out fun but got more disappointing the longer we stayed), Planet Piratez (I think this was an attempt to make pirates cool for today's youth? There were strobe lights and pirate DJs. Didn't really work for me), Planet Pirate Pets (we didn't earn many XP points here, but we did come across some adorable bunnies wearing eye patches), and Continent Cannonball Run (we were disappointed to find that this had nothing to do with pirates, cannonballs, or running).

Slowly but surely, we started building our XP. Along the way, we also discovered a few things:

1. We could pack as much junk as we wanted into our backpacks without filling them up or making them heavy. At one point, I was carrying 23 different types of swords (including four that were on fire), brass boots, iron fists, magnetic mittens, four types of explosives (classic round bombs, sticks of TNT, flash grenades, and an exploding boomerang), a harmonica that put enemies to sleep, a trumpet that called fire from heaven, seven suits of armor, a flamethrower, a random scroll, two hover bikes, and an ice cream cake. Speaking of cake . . .

2. Cake replenishes health in the Reubenverse! Take that, science!

3. There's no nighttime in the Reubenverse, at least, not a regular nighttime (I imagine it's always nighttime

in the Palace of the Dark King). Apparently, there's no need for nighttime when no one needs to sleep. Eric and I planet-hopped for three days straight without getting even a little tired.

Next, let me run through a few planets we visited on our journey:

Planet Trampoline

I love trampolines. I've always said that my first purchase once I get a job will be a trampoline. Planet Trampoline broke me of that real quick. I barfed twice and got my ankle caught in the springs once.

Tiny Town

We were big people in a tiny town. There was a tiny mayor and everything. It was cute. Then we sliced a house open thinking it was a treasure chest and felt bad.

Planet Chocolate

Definitely the low point of our journey. This planet seemed like a no-brainer cupcake. It was not. I mean, there were cupcakes (so many cupcakes), but the world itself was a nightmare of chocolate terrors. Chocolate lava monsters. Chocolate quicksand. Chocolate chupacabras. On top of all that, Eric lost a bunch of XP in the dumbest way possible. He ate devil's food cake and exploded.

Planet Obnoxious Eaters

Another lowlight. We didn't spend a lot of time on this planet because it didn't seem to offer any way to earn XP. I think it was just meant to torture people who committed crimes in the Reubenverse. As soon as we landed, a soundtrack of someone slurping soup started playing, and an indestructible guy chewing with his mouth open began following us.

Planet Ninjas and Sneaky Snakes

It's a good thing Eric and I had beefed up our health before reaching this planet, because during our 35-second stay, we got attacked 297 times. I swung my swords wildly. "WHERE ARE THEY COMING FROM?!" I yelled.

"THEY'RE SO SNEAKY!" Eric yelled back.

We dove back into the pod, huffing and puffing with only 2 percent of our health left. I shared a cake with Eric. "Can we do an easy one next? I don't think we hit one thing back there."

Eric stared past me with wide eyes. "I think we did."

I turned and gasped when I saw a glowing green message.

CONGRATULATIONS! YOU HAVE LEVELED UP.

5,000 XP

CHAPTER 7
Perma-Death

I cracked my knuckles and checked my watch. Three days and six hours left.

"We got this," Eric said as he hit the "Ultimate Warrior Challenge" button.

"Engaging Perma-Death Mode," Siri Lady warned. "Continue?"

"Of course," I said, my voice a little shakier than I'd like.

DING! Fall. *WHOOSH.*

We stepped onto a circular steel arena, probably 100 feet in diameter, floating over a bottomless pit. The pod disappeared as soon as we left it. I gulped and put on my iron fist. Eric pulled a flamethrower out of his backpack. "Let's go!"

As soon as Eric said "go," four little gremlins materialized. (Now, when I say "gremlin," I don't really know if that's accurate. They were ugly green guys with pointy ears, big claws, and no noses. Are those gremlins? I'm not big into mythical creatures.)

Without hesitating, Eric lit up the entire arena with his flamethrower. The gremlins screeched and disappeared.

"Is that all you've got, Max?!" Eric yelled.

"Wave One defeated," Siri Lady said from the clouds.

"Wave One?" I asked. "How many waves are there?"

"Three hundred."

"AHH!" Eric and I screamed in unison. Six more gremlins appeared. Eric continued screaming while he flamed the gremlins.

"Wave Two defeated."

"Hey, Eric?" I asked.

Eric was still screaming, but now it was more of a warrior cry. Ten more gremlins turned into burnt toast.

"Wave Three defeated."

When Eric ran out of breath, I asked my question. "Don't you think you need to cool it on the flamethrower?" .

Twelve gremlins and a dwarf appeared. (Again, it might not have been a dwarf. It was tiny and angry, though. Maybe it was an elf?)

WHOOOOOOSH!

"Wave Four defeated."

"Why? This is the best weapon we have."

Five gremlins and five dwarves appeared. One of the dwarves had a sword.

WHOOOOO . . .

Eric's flamethrower ran out of fuel before he could get the dwarves.

"That's why."

I finished off the dwarves with my iron fist, then Eric took care of the next 17 waves with a sword so long it could be used for pole vaulting. By Wave 22, Eric was so bored that he was just holding the sword out and spinning in circles with his eyes closed. Then—

CRACK!

Eric's eyes popped open. Half his sword lay on the ground, snapped by the rock monster he'd just hit.

"ROOOOAAAAAAR!"

I punched the rock monster as hard as I could with my iron fist. *CRACK!* (That was my fist breaking, not the rock monster, in case you were wondering.)

The monster glared at me. "Help!" I yelled as I started to run. "HELLLLLLP!"

Eric pulled out a Thor hammer and threw it at the rock monster. The monster broke into a thousand pebbles.

"Wave 22 defeated."

Over the next three hours, we faced off against every kind of creature imaginable—elves, dragons, centaurs. There were even unicorns that shot lasers out of their hooves. (You'd think they'd shoot the lasers out of their horns, right? No! That's where they got devious. You'd try sneaking up behind them, then they'd hoof-laser you.)

Slowly but surely, we started losing weapons. We used the last of our flame arrows by Wave 59. Ice arrows were gone by Wave 74. The lightning monsters from Wave 88 shorted out four of our lightsabers. Even the Thor hammer wasn't safe—that got cracked by a knight in chrome armor on Wave 132. Then, on Wave 223, things got really dicey.

"Cake me," I said after getting hit in the shoulder by an acid slimeball.

"I'm out," Eric replied as he battled an ax-wielding toad.

"I know you're out of the chocolate. I'm at 20 percent. At this point, I'll take the coffee cake."

"No," Eric said after kicking the toad off the edge of the arena. "I'm out-out. No more cake."

"Wave 223 defeated."

I got a panic pain in my stomach. "We're not gonna make it!"

"I'm still at 79 percent. We'll be fine."

"You might be fine! There's no way I can survive more than a couple waves on 20 percent!"

"Stay low," Eric said. "I got youuuuuuuuuuuu—"

Right in the middle of Eric's sentence, a skinny brown vine monster snaked out of the ground behind him, grabbed his waist, then grew 30 more feet.

"HEY!" I ran at the vine and swung my sword with all my might. The sword broke in half.

The vine monster held Eric upside down 50 feet above the level and shook him, causing his backpack to open and drop weapons all over the ground. I had to scramble out of the way to dodge Eric's knife collection.

"Use my chain saw!" Eric yelled.

I ran to Eric's chain saw, but the vine creature wouldn't let me kill it that easily. It used Eric as a flyswatter, thwacking him on the ground over and over to squash me. I rolled, grabbed the chain saw, and started the motor in a single motion. I figured I only had two, maybe three seconds to chop down the vine before it dropped Eric and came for me.

I was wrong.

The vine didn't care about me at all. Instead, just as I started sawing its base, it reared back and whipped Eric off the edge of the arena.

CHAPTER 8

Wave 301

I've never been good at thinking on my feet. My brain always provides me with my best comebacks at 3 a.m., which is a totally useless thing for a brain to do. But at that moment, with my best friend's life on the line, my brain came through big-time.

I finished my cut and, without pausing to think, used the vine monster as a giant whip.

THWACK!

Thanks to my bullwhip practice on Handsome Archaeologist Planet, I wrapped up Eric on my first try! Or, at least, I wrapped up his backpack. I yanked as hard as I could, and Eric tumbled back to the arena. His backpack was not quite as fortunate. It tore off his back and went flying with the vine monster off the edge of the arena.

"Wave 223 defeated."

"What are we going to do?!" I yelled as three more vine monsters shot up from the ground.

Eric grabbed the chain saw and ran around the arena, cutting them all before they could grow big enough to kill us.

"Wave 224 defeated."

"We need a superweapon," Eric said.

"We don't have a superweapon."

A spiky-shelled turtle with ninja stars appeared, and Eric grabbed nunchucks from the ground. "We craft one."

"Craft? Like scrapbooking?"

"Scrapbooking?! Are you . . . " Eric jumped as the turtle pulled out its own nunchucks. "Are you serious?!"

"My mom does a lot of scrapbook crafts. You know, with a glue gun."

Eric whacked away the turtle's nunchucks, but before he could finish him off, the turtle pulled out two small ninja swords. Eric groaned. "Video game crafting lets you take two things you've collected and put them together to make something better."

"But how?"

"WHAT?!" Eric yelled, annoyed at either my question or the turtle that'd just sliced his nunchucks in half.

"How do you craft something in here?"

"Crafting is not supported in the Reubenverse at this time," Siri Lady answered from the sky.

"NOTHING CAN EVER BE EASY!"

Eric and I found a way to craft superweapons anyway. Sort of. We started by dumping the contents of my backpack into the middle of the arena with Eric's stuff. Then, we worked together to make the most of the weapons we had left based on the current enemies. For example, Wave 241 introduced giant jelly blobs. I tried throwing a bomb at the first one, but that didn't work— the bomb just bounced off. However, when I tried tossing the bomb to Eric, who hit it with the club, the explosive rocketed off his bat with enough force to reach the middle of the blob's jelly belly and blow it into a million pieces. We'd just invented the Home Run Bomb!

By Wave 254, we'd perfected the Mega Ninja Star, where Eric would pick up two swords, and I'd spin him across the arena with my magnet mittens. During Wave 261, we discovered Knives from the Skies when I accidentally stepped on our makeshift teeter-totter catapult with my brass boots while Eric was setting up. Eric went flying into the air, which gave him the perfect vantage point to whip throwing knives at all the bad guys.

By working together, we actually had an easier time clearing the expert enemies in the final waves than we had with the easy enemies. "Wave 299 defeated," Siri Lady said.

Eric and I cheered, then we saw the final enemy and cheered even louder. It was a jelly blob! Granted, it was bigger than any of the previous jelly blobs by 30 feet, but still, we knew exactly how to take care of it. Eric picked up the club, I tossed him a bomb, and he smashed a home run right into the blob's belly.

KABOOM!

"Wave 300 defeated."

I collapsed on the ground. "Yes, yes, YES!" Eric shouted. He clubbed another bomb off the arena to create a celebratory firework.

"Did the pod come back?" I asked without opening my eyes.

"Not yet," Eric replied.

I breathed with my eyes closed for a few more seconds, then noticed a low rumble. "What's that?"

Siri Lady answered for Eric. "Wave 301."

"WHAT?!" The rumbling got louder. I leaped to my feet, scrambled back to the weapons pile, and grabbed the first thing I could find—the magnetic mittens. Eric held the club over his head. "Bring it on."

WHUMP!

A giant boot materialized to our left.

WHUMP!

Another appeared on our right. Boots that big could mean only one thing. Eric and I both looked up at the same time to see the *new* biggest man we'd ever seen—a 100-foot-tall green giant in full armor.

"AHHHHH!" Before we could do anything besides scream, the giant bent over, scooped us both in one hand, and brought us all the way up to his face. Eric was the first to meet the giant's gaze. He suddenly calmed down. "Closer," Eric said with his club on his shoulder like a baseball bat. The giant squinted.

"Do you have a plan?" I whispered.

Eric nodded slightly. "Closer," he repeated.

The giant brought us closer to get a better look.

"Juuuuust a little closer."

The giant lifted us under his nose and sniffed.

"Good enough!" Eric swung his club. But when he swung, he didn't hit the giant. He hit me.

I flew out of the giant's hand and stuck to his helmet thanks to my magnetic mittens. "WHAT WAS THAT?!" I yelled to Eric.

The giant roared.

"GOOD JOB! KEEP YELLING!"

"Your big plan is yelling in his ear?!" Unfortunately, I didn't have time to learn the answer to that pretty important question because the giant was already swiping at me. I released the magnetic mittens and leaped for the giant's ear. Then I stretched as far as I could, grabbed an ear hair, and held on for dear life.

The giant roared again and started shaking his head like he was trying to get water out of his ear. I crawled up the hair into the ear and tried not to think about how gross this whole thing was.

"AHHHHHHHH!" I screamed the loudest battle cry I could muster while throwing elbows and roundhouse kicks at everything in the ear. Could I bring down a giant from inside his ear? Who knows—I'm relatively sure that I was the first person in history to try.

Suddenly, the whole ear tilted the other way, and I felt weightless. I turned around and poked my head out of the ear. We were falling—not to the ground—but into a bottomless pit.

CHAPTER 9

Error Report

"ERIIIC!"

"Hey," Eric said, giving me a thumbs-up from the giant's nose. He must have hopped over when we'd started falling. "You knocked him over the edge. Nice job."

"WE'RE GOING TO DIE!"

"No, we're not."

I looked up. We were way underneath the arena.

"WE'RE DEFINITELY GOING TO DIE!"

Eric wiggled his eyebrows. "Follow me." He let go of the giant's nose and jumped.

I jumped too, hoping that Eric knew about some special flying ability or something. Nope. We continued falling just above the giant, me screaming my brains out and Eric grinning from ear to ear. I looked down just in time to see a dark fog swallow the giant below us. But before the fog could get us too, everything disappeared in a blinding light.

WHOOSH!

We returned to the all-white room where we'd first met Max.

Eric spread his arms. "Ta-da."

"But, but, but how?"

"In this type of video game, you always win as long as the other guy dies first," Eric explained. "Even if it's by a millisecond."

"Well done!" another voice said.

We both looked up. Max Reuben.

Eric marched up to him. "Forget to tell us about something, buddy?!" He punched right through Hologram Max's stomach.

Max smiled. "Sorry about that extra wave, but true warriors find strength to fight even after they think the battle's been won."

"Or when some fartface decides to change the rules," Eric grumbled.

Max held out his hands, and two trophies appeared. Eric and I did not reach for them. "You have the strength to be an Ultimate Warrior, but strength alone is not enough," Max said. "The strongest man in the world will fail if he does not have the courage to do what is necessary. Do you have a warrior's courage? I believe in you."

"Thanks, fartface."

Max's hologram smiled, then disappeared. As soon as he did, our backpacks reappeared. I peeked in mine to see that the only thing inside was the dumb trophy. The pod materialized behind us, and Siri Lady returned. "What kind of experience would you like today?"

"Courage, I guess," Eric said.

"Sorry, that experience costs 15,000 XP."

I looked at my watch. Two days and 23 hours left. I shook my head. "We need our weapons."

Eric nodded. "Siri Lady, take us to that dinosaur planet."

"Wait, why do you want to go there?"

DING! Fall. *WHOOSH.*

"Welcome to Dino Disaster."

"I want my club back," Eric said as he stepped out of the pod.

"That's a horrible weapon!"

"I like it."

I stopped in my tracks. I thought I heard something.

"And I know you're going to say something about time," Eric continued. "But trust me, we have . . . "

I put my hand over Eric's mouth and dragged him underneath the big leaf of a prehistoric fern. Eric struggled for a few seconds, then he heard it too. It was a man's voice.

"So you're telling me that nobody knows what caused the error."

The voice belonged to Max Reuben.

Eric and I shrank lower and peeked underneath the leaf to see Max walking with two of his henchmen in suits. I could tell this was the real Max because, even though he was still sporting his dumb Thor cape, he was now wearing his signature tucked-in T-shirt underneath.

"We're still investigating," one of the suits explained.

"But someone from the outside was definitely here, right?" Max asked. "What else could have triggered that error?"

"That's possible, sir. We received a Hindenburg alert a few days ago . . . "

"A few days?" Max interrupted.

"Three or four days."

"Four days?!"

The two suits looked at each other. "Right," the second one said. "I know that seems like a long time, but it takes a while to run all the diagnostics."

"I know how long diagnostics take," Max said.

"Of course, but . . . "

"Of course, SIR," Max corrected.

"Of course, sir, I'm sorry, sir. But we, uh, we didn't think it was important enough to bother you."

"Let me remind you of something," Max said. "You're not on Earth anymore. I'm in charge here. Did you know that?"

Both suits fell silent.

"DID YOU KNOW THAT?!"

They both nodded at the same time.

"And because I'm in charge, I get to decide what's important. Not you."

"Yes, sir, and that's why we told you right away," one of them tried.

"Is four days right away?"

When the suit didn't answer, Max pointed to him. The man's eyes got big, he opened his mouth, and he started clutching his throat. Max turned to the other suit. "What's his name?"

"N-Nigel, sir."

"I've revoked Nigel's permission to breathe. Do you think he'd like that back?"

Nigel nodded violently while the other suit looked on in horror.

"Do you think he'd like it back *right away*?" Max wrapped his arm around Nigel's shoulders. "OK, Nigel. I'll get on that right away. You'll be able to breathe again in four days. Sound fair?"

The other suit turned pale.

"NOW TELL ME AGAIN WHY YOU DIDN'T REPORT THIS RIGHT AWAY!"

"I'm sorry! Oh, I'm so, so sorry. It's my fault. The Hindenburg report said that the bug was fixed, so I told Nigel that we didn't need to share it. Of course that's not my decision to make. It's yours, Supreme Ultimate Warrior. Just please let Nigel breathe!"

Max nodded. "Thank you for your honesty." He snapped his fingers, and Nigel gulped air.

Then Max looked back at the other suit. He didn't say anything or even point. He just looked. The suit stared back, too scared to move. Slowly, color started draining from his face. Little cracks appeared all over his body. It eventually became clear that the suit wasn't just scared—he was literally unable to move. After 10 seconds, his entire body had turned gray. Nigel didn't dare say anything, but he looked terrified. Soon, the suit's body appeared so fragile that it could break apart if someone just touched it.

And that's exactly what Max did.

He walked up to the suit, stared in his eyes for a second, and said, "I make the decisions around here." Then he tipped him over with his finger. The man shattered into a thousand pieces.

Max turned to Nigel. "All error reports go directly to me from now on. Understand?"

Nigel was shaking too hard to answer.

Max pressed a few buttons on his watch and started to get pixel-y. Just then, a T. rex jumped out of the bushes and roared. Max snapped his finger. The dinosaur blew up like a balloon and popped. Then Max beamed into the air, and Nigel scrambled into the jungle.

CHAPTER 10

Beans

As soon as the coast was clear, Eric and I sprinted back to the pod and got down to business. We thought that we'd been taking our mission seriously up to that point, but let's be honest—sword-fighting pirates is pretty fun. It wasn't until we saw firsthand what Max was capable of that we really started to focus. Over the next five hours, Eric and I jumped from planet to planet, collecting weapons and building XP with manic intensity. Thanks to all our practice in the strength challenge, we mowed through enemies with ease. There was one small hiccup when we got greedy and challenged the Dark King again only to die instantly, but we rebounded and racked up the extra 10,000 XP we needed.

By the time we returned to the pod and pressed the "courage" button, we had our confidence back.

"Engaging Perma-Death Mode," Siri Lady warned. "Continue?"

"We got this," Eric said.

DING! Fall. *WHOOSH.*

The door opened to reveal that we were suspended midair in the center of a big metal storage building. I peeked over the edge of the pod. Vipers. A room full of deadly vipers. I turned to Eric. "You know how you keep saying, 'We got this'? I wish you wouldn't say that anymore. Like, super-duper wish you wouldn't say that."

The pod began tilting. Eric and I grabbed the doorway to keep ourselves from falling out, but the pod continued to tilt, and our arms got shaky.

Then Siri Lady started counting down. "Ejecting in 3, 2, 1."

WHOOSH!

Just like that, the pod disappeared, and we fell into the snake pit.

"Don't make any sudden movements," I warned.

Eric slowly stood. As he did, the snake nearest him also rose. "You have the flamethrower, right?"

I nodded and reached for my backpack. "It's in my . . . " My heart sunk. "My backpack's gone."

Eric felt his back too. "Oh nooooooooo."

Just then, the biggest snake rose to its full height, hissed, and lunged at Eric's nose.

"NOT THE NOSE!"

Suddenly, we heard a snap and the snake froze.

"Welcome to the second challenge," Max said as he appeared behind us.

"Seriously?!" Eric yelled. He swiped at Max, and his hand passed through. Another hologram.

"This is a test of your heart," Max said. "Can you face your biggest fears? Can you do what needs to be done?"

"Can we skip this?"

Max smiled. "I think you'll learn some interesting things about yourself over the next hour. Resume challenge." Max snapped again, and Eric dodged the snake right before it could bite off his nose.

A snake began wrapping itself around my ankle. I stared it in the eye for 20 full seconds, whispering, "Face your fear, face your fear," the whole time. The snake slithered higher. "Any ideas, Eric?" No answer.

Another viper joined its buddy. "Eric?" I turned. Eric was gone. "ERIC?!"

"Up here!" Eric yelled from above.

I looked up to see Eric swinging on a rope above my head, holding on to something small and furry. "Is that a kitten?!"

"Grab on!"

I jumped and grabbed the rope when Eric came swinging back.

"Kick your feet!" Eric instructed. "Like a swing!" The kitten demonstrated.

I shook the snakes off my legs and swung my feet. After four passes over the snake pit, we reached a hidden platform halfway up the wall. I hooked my legs onto the platform, climbed up, then held the rope for Eric and the kitten. "Where did this come from?!" I asked when all of us were safe.

"I happened to look up, and this little guy was swinging right at me! Can you believe it?!"

No. I couldn't believe it. "You're saying a random kitten was swinging at you like Tarzan? On the very rope you needed to reach safety?"

"It's like a miracle!" Eric sat down and started playing with the kitten. "What's your name, little guy?"

The cat mewed and rubbed its body on Eric. I shook my head. Something didn't feel right here, but I had to admit that the cat was cute. It had huge eyes and a face that was almost too big for its body—kind of like a cartoon.

"I'm going to call you 'Beans,'" Eric said proudly.

"Beans?!"

"Yeah, Beans. You have a problem with that? Beans is a great name for a cat."

"OK, we're not naming it because we're not keeping it. Our deepest, darkest fears are waiting for us at the end of this hallway. I guarantee there are going to be killer clowns, and I'm not dragging Beans into that."

"So you're fine with naming him Beans?"

"We're not naming him anything!"

Eric turned to the kitten. "OK, Beans, Uncle Jesse wants to leave you in the snake room. Do you want to cuddle up and wait for the vicious snakes to build a ladder and eat you alive?"

I looked over the edge of the platform. The snakes were, in fact, crawling on top of each other to build a ladder up to our platform. "Fine," I said. "We find a safe place for him, then we leave him. Understand?"

Eric grinned and held Beans under his arm like a football. Beans snuggled in nice and cozy. "Beans is my best friend," Eric said.

"I'm very happy for you two."

We crept slowly down the dark hallway. There were overhead lights every 10 feet or so, but we still couldn't see very well because most of them flickered creepily.

I kept looking over my shoulder, waiting for a monster to come charging at us. Finally, we arrived at a door. I turned to Eric. "You ready?"

Eric covered Beans's eyes. "We're ready."

I opened the door just a crack, then immediately shut it once I saw what was inside. I felt light-headed.

"Clowns?" Eric asked.

"Yes," I said with my eyes closed.

"No way!"

"Of course there are clowns!" I hissed "Everyone's terrified of clowns."

"Maybe they're friendly clowns."

"They have knives."

"OK, now you're just messing with me," Eric said as he set Beans down. He pushed past me and cracked the door open. Almost immediately, he shut the door and turned to me with huge eyes. "Oh my goodness."

"What do we do?!"

Eric didn't answer because he got distracted by Beans walking back down the hallway. "Hey, bud! Come back here!"

"Shh!" I hissed.

Beans glanced over his shoulder and then picked up the pace. Eric ran after him. "Where are you going, little buddy?"

"Maybe he'd rather take his chances with the snakes."

As Beans continued walking, he paused every 10 feet or so to paw at different sections of the wall. Then, about halfway down the hall, Beans stopped and kept pawing and pawing.

"What do you want?" Eric asked. "Catnip? I can get you some catnip. I know a good catnip guy."

"I don't think he wants anything," I said, examining the panel that Beans was scratching. "He's trying to show us something."

Eric knocked on the panel that Beans was scratching.

BWONG! BWONG! BWONG!

It echoed loudly. Then he knocked on the panel next to it.

THUNK. THUNK. THUNK.

No echo. Beans looked up at us with pride. He'd found a secret passage.

CHAPTER 11

Hypocortezoid Gas

Of course Beans's claws were just the right size to unscrew the wall panel. Of course the panel opened up to a duct just big enough for a person to crawl through. Of course Beans was able to guide us through the branching duct system. The whole thing seemed very . . . convenient.

I tried explaining my growing unease to Eric. "Just listen for a second," I said.

Eric didn't have a second to listen. He was too busy talking to his best friend. "Don't look, Beans. It's too scary for you."

I glanced right. We were crawling next to a vent that let us see into the clown room. "Don't you think it's strange that this magical cat happened to appear the moment we needed help most?"

"Oh man, that one has a chain saw. Tell me you're not looking, Beans."

"Mew."

"Max built this thing himself," I said. "Do you think he just missed a random cat?"

"OK, we're past the clown room. You can look now."

"He has to know about Beans. Maybe he even put Beans here on purpose."

"Oh, look, this room is full of water! Do you like to swim, Beans? I like to—AHHHHH!" A shark interrupted Eric's yammering when it jumped out of the water and rammed its head into the vent.

We scrambled past the shark room, and I tried again. "Max is evil. And if Max put Beans here, then I think we have to consider that Beans could be evil too."

"Now what's this room? Zombies?! Yeesh. Close your eyes again."

"Mew."

As we crawled past rooms full of spiders, skeletons, and saws, I continued trying to talk sense into Eric, and Eric continued ignoring me. Finally, the duct dead-ended.

"Now what?" Eric asked Beans.

Beans put his head down and pushed on the wall.

THUNK!

The panel was so flimsy that our small kitten pushed it over. Again, very convenient. We emerged in front of a door with a big exit sign above it.

"We did it!" Eric exclaimed. I wasn't so sure. Beans seemed downright terrified.

"It's OK, buddy," Eric said. "We're not leaving you behind." That seemed to make Beans even more upset.

We opened the door and stepped inside another one of those white cube rooms that Max seemed to like so much. The only thing inside this one was a small cage on top of a pedestal. "Hello?" I called out. "Max?"

I crept into the room. Eric followed close behind with Beans under his arm. By this point, Beans was shaking like a leaf. As soon as all three of us were in the room, the door slammed shut.

"Max?" Eric called out. "We survived your courage test. Uh, good job on the clowns. Really scary. Can we have our trophies now?"

HISSSSSS!

Something burst in the ceiling, and green gas started pouring into the room. "Get out!" I yelled.

Eric yanked on the door, but it was locked. Gas continued pouring in, slowly covering the ceiling.

"Beans! What do we do?!"

Beans looked sad. Suddenly, the white wall in front of us flickered and turned into a screen showing Max's face. "Made a new friend, I see."

Eric hid Beans behind his back.

"Don't worry. I know that the only way through here is to follow the cat. You've made a wise choice. Now you're going to have to make a courageous one. You see, that's hypocortezoid gas pouring into the room. Hypocortezoid gas is something I invented to put digital bodies to sleep. In three minutes, the room will fill with gas, and you'll fall asleep. Forever." Max paused. "However, there is a choice you can make to save yourself. A courageous choice."

At that moment, the string of coincidences, the impossibly cute cat, and the cage suddenly made sense together. This had been Max's plan all along.

"Courage is all about sacrifice," Max continued. "It's about giving up something good to get something great. You'll never become a true warrior until you've mustered up the courage to sacrifice something that really matters to you. So do you have what it takes?"

Eric looked at me, baffled. "He's very confusing." Then he turned to the screen. "Why don't you say what you mean for once in your life?!"

I felt sick. I knew exactly what Max meant.

Max pointed to us. "I hope you didn't name that cat. It's going to make this next part much more difficult."

"Don't touch Beans!"

"You can get rid of all the gas in the room by simply placing the cat in the cage."

"I'm not doing that," Eric said.

"Eric," I said softly. "You've got to do it."

Eric spun around with a shocked look on his face. "What did you say?!"

"That's not a real cat. It's a video game character programmed to make you fall in love with it so this would be a hard choice."

Eric hugged the kitten to his chest and started backing away. "Don't touch Beans. Don't you dare touch him."

I glanced up. The gas was now covering Max's forehead. "It would be one thing if the cat were real, but just look at those eyes," I said.

Beans looked at Eric with impossibly huge puppy dog eyes.

"No cat has eyes like that. It's like a cartoon. Max is just messing with you. We've got to play his game so we can take him down for real."

Eric had fiery eyes. "Maybe Max did invent Beans . . ."

"He for sure invented Beans."

". . . but I'm not going to play his game. I play by my rules."

I started to panic. "What are you talking about?! You're in the Reubenverse! You play by his rules!"

HISSSSSS!

The gas sounded like it was pouring in faster.

"Ooohooohooo!" Max chuckled and rubbed his hands together. "You still haven't decided? This is getting good!"

My mind raced to figure out an argument that would convince Eric. "He doesn't want you to hurt Beans," I said. "He's just asking you to put a cat in a cage. That's it."

Eric stepped toward the cage and considered it. I glanced up nervously at the gas. Finally, Eric removed his watch and tossed it into the cage.

I waited a moment and breathed a sigh of relief. "See? Nothing to worry . . . "

CHOMP!

The cage suddenly grew teeth and crushed the watch into a million bits.

Eric jumped backward. "YOU STILL WANT TO DO THIS?!"

"I don't. I really don't, but . . . "

"It's like I don't even know you anymore!"

The gas was so low now that it touched my head. I ducked. "It's either us or a fake computer animal!" I said, getting angrier. "That's your choice. And by the way, if you choose the fake animal, you're choosing to doom the entire planet. Just remember that, OK?"

"OK, OK, OK, just let me think," Eric said.

"There's no time to think!"

"There's another secret passage. There has to be." Eric started running, clutching Beans with one arm and feeling the wall with the other.

I took one last look at the gas cloud before gritting my teeth, crouch-running across the room, and tackling Eric.

"OOF!"

The hit caught Eric by surprise and knocked Beans out of his arms. As soon as Beans landed on the ground, he sprinted to the opposite wall. Oh no. I started crawling after him.

"Tsk, tsk, tsk," Max said. The gas had completely covered the screen, but I could still hear his voice loud and clear. "Looks like you weren't courageous enough to do what needed to be done. That's a shame because hypocortezoid gas is nasty stuff."

I kept my eyes on the cat, who was now clawing at the wall.

"Now comes the painful part," Max continued. "The gas will settle in your lungs like . . . "

I tuned out Max so I could concentrate. "Come here, kitty!" I slithered along the ground like a snake. That wasn't getting me where I needed to go fast enough, so I started rolling. I rolled once, twice, three times, then my lungs started burning.

"Eric, hold your breath!" I said. Or at least, that's what I tried to say. Instead, it came out as "Errrrrfffff ffffffffffffffffmmmmmmmmmm" because my mouth had stopped working. I tried again. "Mmmmuuuuhhhhh." My lips felt numb, my head started to cloud, and my lungs felt heavy. So, so heavy. I drifted off to sleep.

NOW LOADING SERVERS ...

CHAPTER 12

System Overload

BEEEEEEEEEEEEEEEEEE

I woke up in a fog. Not an actual fog—that was gone. Instead, my head was swimming with half-memories and blurry images.

EEEEEEEEEEEEEEEEEE

I knew only two things for sure . . .

EEEEEEEEEEEEEEEEEE

. . . that I was soaked from head to toe . . .

EEEEEEEEEEEEEEEEEE

. . . and if that beeping didn't stop soon, I was going to lose my mind.

EEEEEEEEEEEEEEEEEE

I shook my head to clear the fog and found the source of the beeping. It was my watch. I squinted. Two days, 15 hours, and 47 minutes—that was only three hours after we'd entered the courage test. But even though the clock hadn't reached zero yet, the alarm was going off. I unbuckled the watch and threw it across the room.

Next, I sat up and found Eric lying facedown across the room. His arm was still outstretched like he was reaching for me. "Hey, Eric." He didn't move. "Eric!" I felt a twinge of panic in my chest and ran across the room to shake my friend. "Eric, wake up!" I noticed that he was all wet too. I shook him harder. "Come on, wake up!"

Finally, Eric's eyes opened. He stared at me for a second before asking, "Blarg blarggened?"

"What?"

"Mutt mappened? Grut. Blut. What! What shappened?"

I closed my eyes and tried to remember. What had happened? Weren't we supposed to be dead?

Eric sat up and moaned. "Why is it so hot?"

I hadn't even noticed, but it was really, really hot. Wait, were we all wet with sweat? I sniffed my armpit and wrinkled my nose. Definitely sweat.

Eric's eyes snapped open. "Where's Beans?"

"I don't think he made it."

"Beans! BEANS!" Eric jumped and scrambled to the front wall. "BEANS!"

"Eric, I . . . " My voice trailed off when I saw what Eric had noticed. Scratch marks leading to a hole punched through the wall just large enough for a kitten.

Eric poked his head through the hole. "BEANS!"

I peeked inside. It was another all-white room.

Eric shoved me aside and kicked the hole over and over until he tore an opening big enough for us to step through. "We're coming, buddy!"

I cringed as I followed Eric into the next room, bracing myself for the worst. But I didn't have to worry. There was no dead kitty—just two trophies, a collar, and a burnt blue circle on the ground.

Eric picked up the collar. "He saved us," he said quietly.

"You think?"

"Of course. He tore a hole in the wall so the gas could escape before it got to us."

I highly doubted that's what had happened, but since I didn't have a better theory, I kept my mouth shut. I let Eric have his moment of silence, then I picked up a trophy. As soon as I touched it, a warm feeling washed over me, and I beamed into the pod.

"W-w-w-welcome," Siri Lady stuttered. Her face blinked.

A second later, Eric joined me.

"Welllll-ell-ell," Siri Lady tried.

"Well?" Eric asked. "Uh, thank you for asking. I'm not doing too well, actually. You see . . . "

"Siri Lady, what's wrong?" I interrupted.

"Sy-sy-sy-system overload."

The panic twinge returned to my chest. The heat, the alarm, the glitching—it all made sense now. This is what Mr. Gregory had warned us about. I watched the screen helplessly as it cycled from Siri Lady's face to a wall of buttons to an error image. Finally, it settled on a single button: Planet Poodle.

Eric looked at me, shrugged, then pressed the button. The pod dinged a couple of times instead of just once, then we fell for a long time. Finally, the door reopened.

Planet Poodle, as you might imagine, had many, many poodles: pony-size poodles, purse-size poodles, poof-ball poodles, poodles wearing poodle skirts. It also had extremely hot temperatures, a storm on the horizon, and no signs of XP-giving enemies anywhere.

"What are we doing here?" I asked.

Eric shrugged. "It was the only option."

"Yeah, that's cuz the thing was glitching. We need to . . ."

"WHO GOES THERE?!" somebody with a Scottish accent screamed.

I spun around, fully expecting to see a suit pointing a gun at us. Instead, it was a crazy-eyed, scraggly bearded man holding a tree branch over his head.

"Hi. I'm Eric, and this is Jesse."

"HOW DID I GET HERE?!" The man took a threatening step toward us.

Eric and I looked at each other, confused.

"IF I NEED TO CLOBBER SOMEONE TO GET ANSWERS, I'LL START CLOBBERING!" The man took one more step to get within head-clobbering distance and cocked the branch behind his head. I felt for my backpack. Good. It'd returned. I didn't want to fight this guy, but I would if I needed to. Just then, one of the pony-size poodles jumped and grabbed the stick out of the man's hand.

"HEY!"

The dog got down in a playing pose and wagged its tail. Before the man could get his clobbering stick back, Eric and I ran back to the pod.

"CLOSE DOOR!" I yelled as we entered.

The door closed halfway, then got stuck.

Eric and I pushed with all our might to shut the door manually. As we did, I checked outside to see if the lunatic had followed us.

What I saw instead was much more terrifying. The storm on the horizon had gotten closer. Much closer. Close enough that I could now see that those weren't raindrops falling from the sky.

They were people.

CHAPTER 13
Devil's Food

"It started," I said after we'd closed the door.

"What started?"

"That Rapture thing."

"What?!" Eric looked at his wrist, forgetting that his watch had been chomped by a death cage. "I thought we had like two days left!"

"Looks like we slept for two days."

"I've slept for two days before, and I can tell you that was certainly not two days." Eric started to panic. "So how many people are here now? Everybody in the whole world?!"

"Twennnnnnnnnty," Siri Lady answered.

"Twenty people? That's not bad."

Siri Lady wasn't done. "Twenty thousand, four hundred fourteen."

"AHHHHH!"

"Twenty-one thousand, six hundred seven. Twenty-one thousand, nine hundred seventy-two." More buttons began joining Planet Poodle, showing us where people were landing—World of Yodeling Yaks, Liger Lake, and Planet Peeved Porcupines. Siri Lady kept counting. "Twenty-two thousand . . . "

"STOP!" Eric yelled. "What do we do? WHAT DO WE DO?!"

All of the worlds disappeared, then a half of a single grayed-out button flickered onto the screen. "ENDURAN—" it said. Above it was a number. A very large number: 35,000 XP.

I don't know why, but at that moment, I felt calmer than I had all week. Twenty-two thousand people was a lot, but Max still had a long way to go before he sucked everyone into his little game. And 35,000 XP was a big number, but we'd earned big numbers before. We had a mission, and I was determined to continue that mission until the Reubenverse burned down.

"Siri Lady, show us the toughest planets in the galaxy."

The screen made a *fitz* sound, and a wall of buttons blinked on. I nodded to Eric. "We got this."

Over the next half hour, we bounced around to the scariest planets we could find.

DING! "Welcome to World of Warlords."

DING! "Welcome to Magnus the Murder Moon."

DING! "Welcome to Black Hole of the Heart."

DING! "Welcome to Scorpino, Home of the Giant Scorpions."

We didn't even get out of the pod on that last one. As soon as the door opened, a scorpion the size of a dump truck tried jamming its stinger into our pod. "CLOSE DOOR, CLOSE DOOR!" Eric screamed.

The door closed on the stinger tail, which wiggled around in our pod for five terrifying seconds before the scorpion yanked it out. I put my hands on my knees for a moment as I tried to catch my breath. "What's our combined XP now?" I asked.

"Cur-ur-ur-urent commmmmmmm," Siri Lady tried before giving up and just displaying the number on the screen: 19,475 XP.

Eric started taking off his shirt. "It's too hot. We have to get XP quicker."

"Put that back on. I don't want to see your pasty belly."

Eric wrung out his shirt and tied it around his head like a Rambo bandanna, which could not have been more opposite of what I'd asked. "We have to go back to the Dark King."

"And do what?" I asked. "Die in 10 seconds instead of five?"

"I have the flaming sword now. And you have that heavy ax thing."

"There's no way."

We leaned against the wall, sweating and thinking. Suddenly, an idea hit me. "Do we have any more devil's food cake from that chocolate planet?"

Eric looked through his backpack. "Three pieces."

I rubbed my hands together. "Perfect."

"Not perfect. That's the one that makes you explode."

"Right."

"And our whole goal is to kill the Dark King without exploding!"

"Right. *We* don't want to explode because we don't want to lose XP. But now there are a whole bunch of people here who don't care about losing XP." I grinned and waited for Eric to congratulate me on such an awesome idea. Instead, he looked at me with disgust.

"They care about exploding."

"They won't even know it's coming."

"So your plan is—what—grab three people from Planet Poodle, feed them cake, shove them in front of the Dark King, and watch them explode?"

"That's exactly my plan."

Eric gritted his teeth and shook his head like he wanted to say something but was holding it in.

"Listen," I tried. "If you think they need to know up front, I'm sure we could ask for volunteers."

"Stop."

"That guy with the stick seemed like he'd be up for a battle with the Dark King. Maybe we could . . . "

"Stop. Talking." Eric's voice was all shaky.

"You OK?"

"You're not OK," Eric said quietly.

"What?"

Eric got angry. "You are not OK! You're like a different person since we got here. A bad person."

"A bad person? I volunteered to save the world, and now I'm a bad person."

"Yes! Jesse, you wanted to kill a kitten!"

"For the last time, it wasn't a real kitten! It was a computer program!"

"And now you want to kill three innocent people."

"OK, you need to get a grip, Eric. There's a big difference between exploding someone in a fake world where they come back and exploding someone in real life."

"YOU LITERALLY WANT TO BLOW SOMEONE UP!"

"Eric, I'm sorry we have to do things we don't want to do, but this is Max's world. We have to play by his rules."

Eric shook his head. "No, we don't. No. We. Don't."

"Whatever. I'll take care of it myself." With that, I unzipped Eric's backpack.

Eric spun around and grabbed my arm. "Don't you dare," he said with his teeth clenched.

I pulled out a piece of the cake. "Too late." I grinned. "Siri Lady, take us to Planet Poo—" Eric tackled me before I could finish my request.

D-D-D-DING! Fall. *WHOOSH!* "Welcome to Planet Poo!"

"AHHH!" I screamed, both because of the stench and because Eric was biting my arm. I dropped the cake and pleaded with Siri Lady. "Take us somewhere else! Anywhere else!"

DING! Fall. *WHOOSH!* "Welcome to Planet P-p-p-potato Park."

I rolled outside the pod. We seemed to have landed in a potato-themed amusement park. A small potato with a camera around its neck hopped over to me and started trying to take my picture. To my right was a water flume ride where a baked potato boat was splashing down in a river of cream soup. I turned around. "I think we need to . . ."

POW!

I flew backward like I'd been punched by the Hulk. When my head cleared, I looked up to see Eric standing over me, glaring with an iron fist equipped. "I'm going to do this myself. Don't follow me."

I'd been patient with Eric to this point, but he'd crossed a line. "You want to fight?! Then fight like a man." I reached into my backpack and pulled out gloves of my own.

Eric held up his fists. "I'd love to."

I smiled. Eric was in for a surprise—he hadn't seen me pick up these gloves from the black hole planet. I clenched my fists to charge the gloves, and Eric started running at me. The photo potato backed up. He hadn't been trained to deal with something like this. When my fists fully charged, I held them over my head, and Eric lifted off the ground slightly.

"Hey!"

I wasn't done. I pointed one hand at Eric, while I pulled the other back like I was reeling in a marlin.

"Put me down!"

Oh, I'd put him down when I was good and ready. I pulled a little more until he was almost in reach, then I clenched to supercharge the gravity punch.

POW!

I went flying instead. Eric had punched first. The potato looked at both of us, then hopped away as fast as he could.

"That's it!" I pounded my fist into the concrete, which caused the ground to cave in. Then I lifted my arm, and the ground bounced back into place, trampolining me into the air. "AHHHHHHHH!" I screamed like a maniac while supercharging my fist.

"AHHHHHHHH!" Eric yelled while he charged his own fist.

I flew into Eric, and we both punched as hard as we could at the same time.

POWOWOWOWOWOWOWOWOW!

By this point, I'd come face-to-face with a prehistoric sea beast, battled nightmare royalty, and scaled a 10-story giant. I had yet to experience anything with even half the power we created when our fists collided.

First, there was the sound. Our punch had caused a blast so deafening that I couldn't hear anything for a good 10 seconds afterward. Then there was the black hole. The space where our fists had met briefly turned black and almost sucked the skin off my face. Finally, there was the explosion. After a moment, the black hole collapsed on itself and turned into a bright white energy ball that knocked the wind out of my lungs.

After it was all over, I lay on the ground for a few moments with my eyes closed fighting for breath. When I could finally breathe again, I opened my eyes. That's when I saw the tidal wave.

CHAPTER 14

Combo

"RUN!"

Eric and I had accidentally created a blast so powerful that we'd demolished the log flume ride. We ran as fast as we could while the big hill toppled, then dove with our arms outstretched just as the cream soup overtook us. "WHOOOAAAA!" I screamed as I rode the wave. That scream of terror quickly morphed into a scream of glee, however, when I discovered that I could bodysurf on cream soup a lot easier than I could on water. I rode the wave until I bonked my head on the Small Fry Railroad Guy train station.

When I finally stopped, I checked my health. It was still 100 percent! I couldn't believe it! "What was that?!"

Eric stood and wiped the soup out of his eyes. "Combo attack."

I waited for a longer explanation, then followed up when I didn't get one. "Is that a normal video game thing? Like if we combine our attacks, we get something new?"

Eric made a "duh" face at me, then started walking away.

I sloshed after him. "Where are you going?"

"Dark King."

"You think the combo is powerful enough to take down the Dark King?"

"I think it's powerful enough to take down Max."

"Wait!"

Eric turned. "Stop! I'm tired of arguing with you!"

"I just wanted to see if we could swing by the water park real quick to wash the soup off."

Eric rolled his eyes, and we walked to Potato Pond. "Hey, listen. You were right, OK?" I tried after I'd washed off in the wave pool. "There was another way. Obviously, I didn't think of it because I didn't know about combo attacks."

Eric ignored my apology as he wrung the water out of his shirt bandanna.

"If you know about stuff like combo attacks, you need to tell me. We have to work together."

Eric remained silent as he put his shirt back on and dried off inside the air fryer.

"But you have to admit that my idea would have worked too."

Eric walked back to the pod. When I realized he wasn't giving me the satisfaction of a response, I jogged to catch up and almost slipped on a puddle of leftover cream soup.

"Dark King," Eric said when the pod doors closed.

DING! Fall. *WHOOSH!*

We reappeared in the throne room, and the Dark King looked at us like, "Oh brother, you two again?" I started sweating more than ever. The king cracked his knuckles and stood up. By my calculations, we had four seconds before he started pointing.

One-one-thousand.

Eric ran behind the throne. I clenched my fists to start charging the gloves.

Two-one-thousand.

The king smiled and lifted his arm. The screeching violins started.

Three-one-thousand.

The king pointed at me. I put my head down and ran toward Eric.

Four-one-thousand.

I jumped-punched at the same time Eric did. Our fists connected just as the king shot his black beam.

POWOWOWOWOWOW!

The king's attack only fueled our black hole, causing it to grow and grow. For a moment, the Dark King looked at the hole, confused. Then his face started to warp as his skin got sucked in. He tried scrambling backward, but he was too late—the hole exploded in a burst of light, swallowing the Dark King whole.

DING DING DING!

Bells chimed as our XP meters filled up.

"Woo-hoo!" I celebrated and danced. Even Eric took a break from his moping to crack a smile. We ran back to the pod. "What's our XP?"

The number 42,221 appeared on the screen.

"Take us to the endurance challenge!" I yelled.

"Engage Perma-Perma-Perma—" Siri Lady got stuck in a Perma-Death loop.

"Yes! Do it!" Eric yelled as he banged on the wall.

Ding! Fall. *WHOOSH!*

The doors opened, and there was Max in another white room. He spread his arms. "Welcome, warriors."

This time, Eric didn't even try to punch him.

"Ultimate Warriors aren't just strong in body and heart; they also have strong spirits. This might be your toughest challenge yet, but I'll be waiting for you if you endure to the end."

BING! A red square appeared on the wall in front of us.

"This is you," Max explained.

BING! A green square appeared next to it.

"And this is where you need to go. Simple enough, right? I'll even show you the way."

The squares started shrinking, and lines began appearing all over the walls as well as the floor and ceiling. It almost looked like we were zooming out on something. Once the two squares had shrunk to the size of postage stamps, a dotted line snaked around the room, connecting the red square to the green square. That's when I realized what we were looking at. It was a maze. And not just any maze, but possibly the longest maze ever constructed.

Max was beaming. "It's a maze! The longest maze ever constructed."

I groaned. We were bad at mazes. Specifically, Eric was very, very bad at mazes. Any time a teacher would give our class a maze activity when we were little, Eric would connect the start and finish dots with a line outside the maze. Last year, a few families in our neighborhood tried a corn maze together. After three minutes of wandering, Eric panicked and ran through row after row of corn until someone dressed up as a scarecrow kicked him out.

"If you follow this exact path, you should be able to finish the maze in eight days."

My heart sank. Days? Did he say "days"?

"I hope you've been getting a good look at the map, because this is the last you'll see of it. It disappears in three . . . "

"No, wait! I have a camera!" Eric shouted as he dug through his backpack.

"Two. One."

Eric pulled out his camera just as the map vanished into the white walls.

"The good news is you shouldn't die in here," Max said. "The bad news is you'll probably lose your mind. Good luck!"

NOW LOADING SERVERS ...

CHAPTER 15

Glue Gun Crafting

Max disappeared, and the front wall lowered to reveal a hallway forking into five paths. Eric pulled a sledgehammer out of his backpack and started pounding the wall behind us.

CHUNK! CHUNK! CHUNK!

I sighed. "What are you doing?"

CHUNK! CHUNK! CHUNK!

The sledgehammer bounced off the wall like it was made of rubber, so Eric tossed it aside and pulled out a pickax.

CHINK! CHINK! CHINK!

"This is going to be pretty miserable if you don't start talking to me," I said.

CHINK! CHINK!

I grabbed Eric's pickax before he could swing it again. "Hey! I asked what you're doing!"

"I'm getting us out of here!"

"Really? Cuz it looks like you're trying to break an unbreakable wall."

Eric turned. Sweat was dripping down his face. "If you were paying attention, you'd remember that the end of the maze is on the other side of this wall. So if we break through, we win. Got it?" He snatched the pickax back.

CHINK! CHINK! CHINK!

Of course, Max wouldn't have shown us the map if there were any way to break the wall. In fact, he'd probably put the start and finish so close together on purpose to drive people even crazier. If we were going to survive the next eight days, we couldn't waste energy on dumb stuff like this.

I wiped the sweat off my forehead. Man, it was hot. Something about the maze was trapping heat big-time. Maybe it was the enclosed hallways, or maybe it was the reflective walls, but the maze felt twice as hot as anywhere else we'd been.

CHINK! CHINK! CHINK!

I couldn't wait for Eric any longer. I started walking down the hall. "Hey!" Eric yelled. "Where are you going?!"

"If you run your hand along the right wall, you can solve any maze," I said.

"Are you crazy?!" Eric shouted. "That's gonna take forever!"

"You can catch up once you're done fooling around. I'll just be—YOWZA!" I jerked my hand back as soon as I touched the wall. It was at least a thousand degrees. No worries, I could just follow the wall with my eyes. I continued walking.

Squish. Squish.

"Hey, Jesse?"

Squish. Squish.

"Jesse."

Squish. Squish.

"Jesse!"

"WHAT?!"

"You're leaving footprints."

I turned to see a trail of black tar footprints behind me. Weird. I checked the bottom of my shoe and—oh no. Ohhhhhh no. I hadn't stepped in anything black— my shoe was black! The floor was melting my shoes! Once my soles were gone, nothing would be left to separate my feet from the lava ground. I ran back to Eric.

Squishsquishsquishsquish.

"Start swinging!" I yelled as I grabbed the sledgehammer.

CHINK! CHUNK! CHINK! CHUNK!

"Wait!" I set down the sledgehammer. "Let's try the combo attack!"

Eric started charging his iron fists. I clenched my gravity gloves. Once they fully charged, I counted down from three and punched Eric's fist with all my might.

POWOWOWOWOWOWOW!

Nothing. And now my shoes were getting soupy.

"Dump out your backpack!" Eric commanded as he emptied his.

We started sorting through the junk. Over the past week, we'd accumulated tons of random stuff. There was a Reubenverse flag, a beanbag chair, a party-size tub of cottage cheese (who throws a party with cottage cheese?), a World War II helmet, a . . .

"What's that?"

"Oh, that's a jet engine," Eric said.

"Why did you keep a jet engine?"

Eric shrugged. "In case we found a jet, I guess."

I sat on the beanbag chair and put my head in my hands. Nothing we'd collected could come close to breaking through the wall. And if we weren't getting through the wall, we weren't getting out of the maze. I cleared my throat. I figured if I was going to cook in a horrible video game maze oven, I should probably make things right with my best friend.

"Hey, Eric, I . . . "

"I know," Eric interrupted.

"It's just . . . "

"It's OK," Eric said.

I looked up. Eric was smearing a melting Wiffle ball around on the ground. "I mean it," I said.

"I do too."

I felt like we should hug or something to finalize things, but there was no way I was going to cross the lava floor, so I just nodded at Eric. He nodded back.

I sat for a few more seconds before the smell of melting vinyl beanbag got to be too much, then I looked around for my next place to sit. That's when I noticed something weird about the jet engine.

"Why is that melting?" I asked.

Eric looked at the misshapen engine. "The outside's probably made of a light metal. Light metals melt easily."

"That sounds like a dumb choice for a jet engine."

Eric shrugged. "Aircraft use lots of light metals."

"What, are you a pilot or something now?"

"I know lots about aircraft."

Suddenly, my eyes got big. "Craft!"

"Huh?"

"We can craft now!"

Eric squinted at our pile of junk. "No, we can't."

"Maybe not nerdy video game crafting, but definitely mom-with-glue-gun crafting!" I used a small parachute to shuffle over to the engine without burning my feet. I rolled the engine over and nodded my approval when the bottom kind of stuck to the floor. "We use the ground as our glue gun to get the metal hot enough that it'll stick to something else!"

"Like what?" Eric asked.

I pushed the jet engine until it chinked into the sledgehammer. Eric's eyes lit up. "Rocket-powered sledgehammer!"

We immediately got to work on our new creation by superheating one side of the jet engine. Then, we carefully rolled it over and smooshed the hammer on top. The hammer sunk in with a satisfying *SQUISH*. We waited a bit to let it set, then tried wiggling the handle. Not too bad! We smeared melty shoe tar and plastic around the bond to strengthen it, waited a few more minutes, and tried again. Perfect!

I flipped three switches on the engine.

VROOOOOOOOM!

The sledgehammer rattled in my hands. I tightened my grip, cocked it behind my shoulder, and swung with all my might.

CHUNK.

Instead of bouncing off the wall like before, the sledgehammer got a little stuck. My heart raced. I pulled it out and swung again.

CHUNK. CHUNK. CRACK!

On the third swing, I cracked a hole in the wall just big enough to peek through.

Eric checked it out first and pumped his fist. "I knew it!"

I looked, too, and grinned. The room was all green. Eric backed up, and I smashed a hole big enough to step through.

"Hi, Max! We're here!" Eric yelled as he walked into the room.

"Conggggggratulationszzzzz," Max said. We spun around to find his glitching face on the wall we'd just smashed through. Our hole was right where his mouth should have been. "I did-id-id-idn't think yoowoowoowoowoo . . . "

The screen zapped black and went silent. We waited for a moment. Was it broken? Then, the room flashed blue.

It took me a moment to remember where I'd seen a blue flash before, but when I did, I gasped out loud.

"What is it?" Eric asked.

"We need to get out," I whispered.

"But . . ."

I pushed Eric back through the hole. "Now!"

We scrambled out of the room and hid around the other side of the wall—me on the right side of the hole and Eric on the left. I stood perfectly still and tried to catch my breath without gasping too loudly.

Eric held up his arms. "What?" he mouthed.

I tapped my ear. *Listen.*

Ten, twenty, thirty seconds went by. Silence. Then, I heard it.

The unmistakable sound of gas mask breathing.

CHAPTER 16
The Potato Sack Hop

When we broke the wall, we broke the Reubenverse. And when we broke the Reubenverse, we broke our pact with the Hindenburg. We were no longer pals to be protected. We were now bugs constructing overpowered weapons to destroy Max's perfect prison. That made us the enemy.

I sneaked a peek inside the green room. The Hindenburg was slowly walking around, inspecting the walls with its tentacles.

Scraaaaaaaaaape.

Eric started using his foot to scoot a lightsaber closer to him. I held a finger up to my mouth. *Shhhhhh!* We held our breath and listened. Suddenly, a loud voice broke the silence. Max's voice.

"You thought you were d-d-d-done!"

I jumped a mile.

"I h-h-h-ave ooooooooooooone more . . ."

I looked at Eric. He looked at me. Suddenly, a third head appeared in the hole between us. The Hindenburg.

"AHHHHH!" In a blind panic, I picked up the nearest object and swung as hard as I could.

POW!

Fortunately, the nearest object happened to be the rocket-powered sledgehammer. I connected with the Hindenburg's face and sent it flying back into the green room.

"GO! GO! GO!"

Eric and I ran down the hall toward the forking paths. With five different paths, we had an 80 percent chance of picking a different one from the Hindenburg.

Squishsquishsquishsquish.

I looked down to see that our chances of picking a different path had shrunk to zero. We were leaving a footprint trail that would lead the Hindenburg directly to us. Suddenly, I had an idea. I grabbed the Reubenverse flag from the ground and kept running.

Squishsquishsquishsquish.

"He's gonna know where we are!" Eric panicked.

"No, he's gonna know where our footprints are," I corrected as I turned down the left hallway.

"THAT'S THE SAME THING!"

Squishsquishsquishsquish.

I stopped Eric after we rounded the first corner, and I spread the flag on the ground like a blanket. "Hop on."

"Ohhhhhhh."

We shuffled as fast as we could. If we could get to another hallway without leaving tracks, we'd buy ourselves a few extra minutes. I kept nervously glancing at the green room hole, waiting for the Hindenburg to reemerge. We weren't shuffling fast enough. I finally pulled up the flag's corners. "Potato sack!"

Eric followed my lead, and we potato-sack-hopped to the far-right hallway before the Hindenburg returned.

"Now what?" Eric mouthed after we'd made it safely around the corner.

I pointed back toward the green room. Eric shook his head violently. I nodded. Running for the green room might expose us to the Hindenburg, but at least it'd give us a little hope. I peeked to make sure the Hindenburg had followed our tracks down the left hallway, then ran.

Squishsquishsquishsquishsssssssssssssssss.

I choked back a yelp. My shoe sole had finally melted all the way through, and I was now basically running on hot coals. I tried to picture myself running over ice cubes instead.

"YOWWWWWWW!"

I turned to see Eric holding his left foot. Apparently, he had not used my ice cube trick. Behind Eric, the Hindenburg emerged from the left hallway with its blaster aimed at us.

"Hurry up!" I yelled. Eric ran around me, and I picked up a shield from our pile of junk.

BLAST!

My shield disintegrated. I picked up another one and kept running.

BLAST!

My second shield disintegrated too. I picked up one last shield before diving into the green room.

BLAST!

The third shot passed right through the shield. Fortunately, it also went over my head.

"I loooooooook ffffffffffforward," the Max video said behind me, still struggling to finish the speech.

"Move over!" Eric yelled.

I looked up to see Eric standing in the middle of the room with his T-shirt tied around his foot, spinning our rocket sledgehammer faster and faster. I rolled out of the way just as the Hindenburg burst through the wall and Eric let the hammer fly. This time, the alien was ready for it. The Hindenburg simply reached out a tentacle, caught the hammer, and crunched it into rubble.

Eric, to his credit, was not fazed at all. He charged his fist while staring down the Hindenburg.

"Find it qu-qu-quite enliiiiiiiiiightening," Max continued.

I quietly charged my fist too. If we timed things right—

GACK!

Without shifting its gaze from Eric for even a second, the Hindenburg shot out its left tentacle and grabbed my throat. I gulped for air, but the grip was too tight.

"Heeeeeeeeeeeeeeeeere," Max said.

My fist finished charging. If I could just keep it clenched, maybe we could still try the combo punch. Eric took a step forward, and the Hindenburg tightened its grip even more. My head felt like it was going to pop off my shoulders.

"Issssszzzzzzzzzzzzzz," Max continued, his voice breaking up.

Eric raised his fist. The Hindenburg wrapped even more of its tentacle around my head. Blackness took over my vision.

"Your re-re-re-rewarrrrrrrrrrrrrrrd," Max finished.

DING!

In one last effort before losing consciousness, I limply swung my fist back and forth.

POWOWOWOWOW!

Eric jump-punched and connected with my fist. Black hole. Crawling skin. I waited for the Hindenburg to loosen its grip. White energy burst. Thunderclap. The Hindenburg barely flinched.

The key word in that sentence is "barely."

Because the Hindenburg did flinch. Just a little. And that little flinch was all I needed to gulp a lungful of air and regain my vision.

When I could see again, I found two trophies just out of reach to my right. Eric grabbed one and disappeared. Before the Hindenburg could retighten its grip around my neck, I put everything I had into swinging and squirming and shimmying toward the trophy. That effort, combined with the slippery sweat covering my body, gave me the final few inches I needed to touch the trophy with my bare toe.

It felt cold. Then, it disappeared.

NOW LOADING SERVERS ...

CHAPTER 17

Trust Nothing

GAAAAASP!

I grabbed at the tentacle around my throat while trying to fill my lungs with air.

"Jesse!"

GAAAAASP!

I kicked and thrashed harder. If I could just get the Hindenburg to let up a little . . .

"Jesse! Snap out of it!"

I opened my eyes to see Eric standing over me.

"I'm . . . choking," I wheezed.

"No, you're not. We teleported."

I felt my neck again. Eric was right—the tentacle was gone, but my windpipe still felt like it was getting crushed. I tried a test swallow, then took a few deep breaths. Everything seemed normal. Finally, I squinted at Eric. Whoa. Not normal. "What in the world are you wearing?"

Eric tugged on his black jumpsuit. "You're wearing the same thing. Apparently, it's our uniform here."

I sat up to see where "here" was and gasped when I saw an enormous castle from the future stretching into the sky. It looked like someone couldn't decide whether they wanted to build a castle or a skyscraper, so they settled on Frankensteining together this 1,000-foot glass-and-metal monstrosity.

"Welcome to Planet Max!" Max's voice boomed from the sky. "I have one final test for you. Actually, it's more of a lesson."

I stood up to get a better look at our surroundings. Max's castle of doom was situated on top of an island floating over a bottomless pit. Red clouds swirled overhead. And though the temperature wasn't quite oven-level like the maze, it was still really hot.

"You've proven yourselves worthy warriors through tests of strength, courage, and endurance," Max continued. "But to get the most out of your ability, you need one final skill. It wasn't until I learned this skill myself that I became an Ultimate Warrior. Today, you, too, will become an Ultimate Warrior because today, you will learn wisdom."

If Eric and I could roll our eyes any farther, we'd be looking at our brains. We just wanted to find Max, not listen to some weird lecture on the art of war. Unfortunately, all Max wanted to do was deliver weird lectures on the art of war.

"Lesson number one: Trust nothing," he said. "The system was built to keep you down. A true warrior doesn't take the path marked for him. He doesn't trust it. He makes his own path. He opens his own doors."

We waited for more pearls of wisdom, but Max seemed to be done for now. "Thanks, Confucius," Eric grumbled as he reached for the handle of the 20-foot castle door.

HISSSSS!

Without warning, an angry black eel shot out of the door's keyhole and latched on to Eric's hand.

"HELP!" Eric screamed as he flailed.

I tried helping from a distance by yelling at the eel. When that didn't work, I edged closer and karate-chopped the eel's back. The creature finally let go when Eric landed a roundhouse kick.

"You OK?" I asked.

Eric grimaced as he rubbed a growing black welt on his hand. "It really burns."

I stared at the door. What were we supposed to do? I certainly wasn't going to get near that keyhole again. Then I remembered Max's words. "There's another way in," I said.

"Huh?" Eric asked, still annoyed about the eel.

"A true warrior opens his own doors. There's a secret way in."

Eric looked at the sky as he continued to rub his hand. "This is my least favorite video game of all time."

I looked around. How does one find a secret passage, anyway? Maybe there was a fake bush we had to pull? A misshaped brick to push? A shovel for tunneling?

Eric had a different idea. He stood in front of the door (far out of range of the keyhole eel) and kicked as hard as he could.

"HIYAAAOWWWWW!" Eric's karate scream turned into a yelp of pain when his foot passed through the door, dropping him straight onto his butt.

I stepped over Eric and through the totally fake door. "Amazing," I whispered.

Just inside the door was an umbrella stand filled with swords. "TAKE ONE," a sign read. I grabbed a curved sword that looked like one of my favorites from Planet Pirate. Eric went for the biggest sword he could find. It immediately turned into an eel that bit his hand.

"I HATE EELS SO MUCH!"

I cut the eel in half, then helped Eric pick a sword that wouldn't bite him. We stepped through the welcome foyer into the main tower.

"Unnnnnnng," I groaned.

As tall as Max's castle looked from the outside, it felt even bigger inside. Never-ending flights of stairs wound around the tower and crossed overhead at impossible optical-illusion angles. There were doors too. Lots of doors. Doors at the top of stairs, doors at the bottom of stairs, doors hung crooked halfway up the wall like one of those Dr. Seuss illustrations where he draws ridiculous buildings no one could ever use.

We took a second to gather ourselves. "Shall we?" Eric asked, as he grabbed the handle of the nearest door.

You'll never guess what the handle did.

"WHY IS EVERYTHING AN EEL?!"

I sliced the eel, then Eric kicked down the door. "I'm getting awfully sick of—AHHHHH!"

A gorilla-sized reptile with bony arms lunged at the door. Eric jumped backward into me, which caused us both to fall. The creature moved so fast that we didn't have time to do anything but lie on our backs and kick our legs. Not like that could possibly protect us against such a humongous . . .

"RAAAAAWWWWWWwwwwwwwwrrrr."

Eric landed a kick to the creature's stomach, causing it to fly around like an untied balloon. It did three laps around the room, then popped in a cloud of yellow smoke near the ceiling.

We stared in disbelief for a moment before Eric rolled off of me. "Trust nothing, I guess."

That would have been a good lesson for us to carry into the next room, where a small Furby-looking critter waited. "Hey, buddy," I said as we walked by. "We're just—AHHHHH!"

The Furby pulled a samurai sword out of nowhere and nearly sliced off my head. When Eric tried to help me, the creature whipped out a second sword and battled both of us at once. After 20 minutes of sword fighting (which feels like 20 hours of any other activity), we finally escaped.

As you might imagine, our nerves were beyond frayed when we opened the next door. No monsters in this room. Everything was just upside down.

I lost track of time as we slowly—ever so slowly— worked our way up Max's nightmare castle. It was like . . . have you ever been to a haunted house? I've only been once, and that wasn't even on purpose. At our town's Fall Fest a few years ago, an older kid named Oscar showed Eric and me a door that he claimed would lead to a trick-or-treating fun house. Turns out, Oscar was a jerk. The door actually led to a haunted mansion that seemed to stretch for miles. Every step was the new most terrifying step of our lives because we didn't know what new creature was going to jump from the shadows and scream in our faces. By the time we stumbled through the exit, we were wet noodles of emotion. Imagine our surprise, then, when we turned around to see that the "mansion" we'd conquered was actually just three dinky trailers strung together.

My point is: The human brain can handle only so much suspense and surprise. When you're constantly peeking around corners for bogeymen or waiting for the next trap to spring or testing doorknobs for eels, your mind starts to break down. So when we finally heard Max's voice again, we welcomed it like the return of an old friend.

"Congratulations, warriors," Max said after we'd crossed a piranha pool on a rickety invisible bridge. "You're ready for your final lesson. Follow me."

A blue line appeared on the ground. It snaked around the room and led to a glowing door that had appeared on the opposite wall. I breathed a sigh of relief. Would I usually just waltz into the lair of a psychopath? Certainly not. But Eric and I were so glad to finally step through a door without testing it for eels that we threw it open with glee. Past the door, the blue line took us up a staircase, through a secret passage, and into a large, round room with a domed ceiling. The line ended at two folded papers lying on the ground.

I picked up the first paper. "Lesson number two," I read aloud. "Trust no one."

Eric unfolded the second paper. "Even me."

CREEEAAAK!

I looked up just in time to see the ceiling begin to crumble. We made it two steps back toward the door before the ceiling collapsed on top of us.

CHAPTER 18

Trust No One

"So close."

I rubbed my head in confusion. One second, Eric and I had been getting crushed under a pile of rubble. The next, we were sitting across a conference table from Max. Max shook his head like he was disappointed. "So, so close."

I rolled my chair back from the table and spun slowly. We seemed to have gone back in time. The room was filled with hundreds of those six-foot-tall punch card computers from the 1970s. There was also orange carpet, old-timey desks, and the smell of cigarette smoke. The only thing telling me we were still in the Reubenverse was the sweat that continued to drip down my forehead.

"Trust nothing," Max said. "'No one' is included in 'nothing.' I hoped you would have figured that out on your own." He sighed. "But since you didn't, I'm going to have to teach you."

Eric reached across the table and tried to slap Max. His hand went right through Max's face. He sighed and plopped back down.

"I've re-created, down to the last carpet stain, the room where I finally became a warrior." Max leaned back and spread his arms. "Today, this is a floor in my San Francisco skyscraper, but back in 1978, I didn't own the whole building. I didn't even own the whole floor. My best friend and I rented just a small corner of this room to start our first business together."

"UHHHHHHGGGGG." Eric let out a long sigh that lasted for Max's last two sentences.

"We didn't have fancy equipment, we didn't have much education, and we certainly didn't have a lot of money. But we had each other. More important, we had an idea. A great idea. Do you want to hear it?" He paused for dramatic effect. *"Pizza Boy."*

"UHHHHHHGGGGG," Eric repeated and he stood up. "I'm leaving. Let me know when he's done."

"We were video game developers before that was even a job. And our big game was *Pizza Boy*. *Pizza Boy* was brilliant. It was about a kid who loved pizza so much that he'd sneak into a haunted pizzeria at night to eat all their pies before the Italian ghost chefs could catch him. We worked so hard on that game. I stayed up through the final three nights to finish the animation. It was a masterpiece." Max looked sad. "It was our masterpiece."

I wanted to tell Max that he didn't need to be so sad because *Pizza Boy* definitely didn't sound like a masterpiece, but I saved my breath. He couldn't hear me anyway.

"After that third all-nighter, we threw a little party for ourselves. Dr Pepper got us through those long nights, so we toasted with those glasses of Dr Pepper you see on the table." Max pointed to the two half-full glasses in front of me. "That morning, my partner hopped on a plane to sell the game to an arcade manufacturer in Japan. He promised that he'd call as soon as the sale went through. I waited next to the phone all day. It never rang. Of course it takes longer than a day to sell a game, right? I gave him a week. Nothing. Maybe a month? No call. In fact, I never spoke to or saw him again. Do you know what I did see again?"

This was the most emotional I'd ever seen Max. I could tell this story still really meant something to him.

"*Pizza Boy*. I saw *Pizza Boy* at the arcade. Mind you, it wasn't called *Pizza Boy*. The pizza theme was totally gone. But the main character looked the same, the ghosts acted the same, and the levels played almost identical. The biggest thing that had changed was the name. The new name was *Pac-Man*."

Ohhhhhhh. OK, now that I thought about it, *Pizza Boy* did sound a lot like *Pac-Man*. Now it made sense why Max would be so upset. He felt like he'd invented the most popular game of all time only to have it stolen by his best friend.

"I fought for years to get my creation back, but nobody would believe me. Eventually, I learned the lesson that I hope to teach you: If you want something, you've got to get it yourself. As a warrior, you have no friends. You only have allies. You and your ally have used each other to get to my castle. That's good. Now, it's time to be great."

Floating balls appeared with an old arcade *BLOOP* sound effect. Just then, Eric sprinted around the corner. "The computers are set up in a maze!" Then his eyes got wide when he saw the floating balls. "It's the *Pac-Man* maze!"

"Your final test is *Pizza Boy* the way it was meant to be played," Max said. "In this game, the ghosts are not your enemy. Your partner is. The game only stops when one of you dies. And just so you know, I've programmed death by ghost to be the most painful thing anyone could ever experience."

BLOOP-BLOOP-BLOOP!

The sound of ghosts started closing in.

"One more thing," Max said. "I've added a small mercy to this version of the game. If you're having trouble pushing your partner in front of a ghost, simply drink one of the Dr Peppers on the table. Your partner will die instantly and painlessly. OK, warriors. Claim your prize." With that, Max disappeared.

Eric and I stared at each other in shock for a second. Then, Eric dove for the soda.

NOW LOADING SERVERS ...

CHAPTER 19

Pizza Boy

"WAIT!" I jumped out of my chair and grabbed for the glass before Eric could drink.

Eric snatched the glass away. "I'm not gonna let you kill me!" he said as he dumped it out.

I stared at him dumbfounded. "You actually think I'd drink that?"

Eric dumped the second glass too. "I don't know anymore."

"Eric, I would never . . . "

BLOOP-BLOOP-BLOOP!

A red ghost cut my explanation short when it emerged from the computer maze to my left. I pushed my rolling chair into the ghost to slow it down, but the chair went straight through because—duh—it was a ghost. I joined Eric and ran through another opening in the maze.

"You have to know I would never do that to you," I tried again.

"You're all about following his rules, right?"

"Come on, Eric."

"The rule is that one of us has to die. Well, who's it gonna be, huh?"

BLOOP-BLOOP-BLOOP!

A pink ghost emerged in front of our faces. We doubled back, then turned down another hallway.

"He's lying again, you know," Eric continued. "There's another way out."

I nodded, even though I knew in my heart that Eric was wrong. Eric hadn't heard Max's story. He hadn't seen the emotion. The *Pizza Boy* thing meant a lot to Max—maybe more than anything that had ever happened in his life. The whole Warrior Challenge had been building to this moment. Max had designed his challenge for teams because he needed to teach this one final lesson.

Suddenly, Eric slammed on the brakes. "I have an idea! Give me a boost!"

I boosted Eric on top of the computer towers, then he helped me up just as the blue ghost arrived. Soon, the other three ghosts joined up and started circling our location. It was creepy, but at least the four ghosts were too short to reach us. While I caught my breath, I took a moment to check out the room. It was a big square just like the room with Mr. Gregory's computer tower from the real world. Actually—maybe it was the room from the real world.

Eric interrupted my thoughts by pointing to the blue ghost, which now had one arm. "We've got a problem."

I watched in horror as the ghost sprouted a second arm that grew long enough to reach the top of our tower. "GO, GO, GO!"

Eric and I took off just as the blue ghost pulled himself up. We raced along the towers until two more hands appeared ahead. I grabbed Eric and tumbled to the ground just as the pink ghost pulled itself up. Then I stood up, took two steps, and—"OOF!"—tripped over one of the extension cords snaking along the ground. Eric turned to help me up, but the pink ghost jumped between us.

"SPLIT!" Eric yelled.

I ran left, and Eric ran right. The pink ghost chose me.

BLOOP-BLOOP-BLOOP!

Even though I was running as fast as I could, he was still gaining. I put my head down and pushed harder. My chest felt like it was on fire.

BLOOP-BLOOP-BLOOP!

Tears started coming when I realized that we were out of options. One of us had to die, and that was that. I decided that it would be me. Just as I was about to give myself up to the ghost, I tripped over another cord.

"OOF!"

BLOOP-BLOOP—

Silence.

I looked up. The ghost was no longer pink. Instead, it was bright blue and had a scared face. Behind the ghost was Eric. Wearing a chef's hat.

"PIZZA BOY TO THE RESCUE!"

Eric easily overtook the ghost and tackled it. The ghost disappeared with a *BLING!*

"That was unbelievable!" I said.

"Pizza Boy never leaves a soldier behind."

"What happened?"

"I picked up a slice of pizza and got this sweet hat."

Just then, the hat started blinking. Another blue ghost peeked around a corner.

"Get back!" Eric yelled. He dove at the ghost, and it disappeared with another *BLING* just before Eric's hat vanished for good.

"So we just find more pizza and kill all the ghosts!" I said.

"The pizza doesn't kill them; it just sends them back to the middle of the maze," Eric said. "Haven't you ever played *Pac-Man*?"

I ran alongside Eric for a few seconds before speaking up again. "You know one of us is going to have to die, right?"

"Stop talking like that!"

The orange ghost rounded the corner in front of us. We turned around. The red ghost appeared behind us. Eric ducked down a side hallway and reappeared with the chef's hat. I waited patiently while he ran after the two ghosts screaming and waving his arms. "I want it to be me," I said when he returned.

"Pizza Boy never . . . "

"Eric, come on," I interrupted.

Eric grabbed me. For the first time, he looked truly scared. "There's another way, OK? You can't give up."

"You'll have a better chance against Max. You're better at . . . "

"STOP!" Eric clenched my arm tighter. "I'm not letting go until we get out of here, do you hear me?"

He got two steps down the hallway before tripping over a power cord. "These stupid, stupid . . . "

My eyes lit up. "Power cords!"

"They're the worst," Eric said as he kicked at them.

"No, I have an idea! The power cords need to go somewhere, right?"

"Yeah. The wall."

"No, I mean, there are a ton of cords here. You need something big to handle all that power."

Eric shook his head like he didn't get it.

"I think this room is a replica of the one Mr. Gregory is in right now. Remember how he said he could shut down the power?"

Eric's eyes lit up. "That electric box!"

"Right! I'll bet we can shut this whole thing down if we just find it!"

"YES!"

BLOOP-BLOOP-BLOOP!

The pink and orange ghosts rounded the corner in front of us, while the blue and red ghosts cut off the route behind us. They were starting to work together.

"Boost me!" Eric said.

I shoved Eric on top of the computers, then he helped me up just in time. We had only a few seconds to scan the room. Come on, come on, come on . . . "There!" I pointed to the metal box in the far corner.

"And there's a pizza slice!" Eric yelled, pointing down below.

We hopped off the tower and made a beeline for the pizza slice. Eric grabbed it, turned, and karate-chopped two ghosts.

"HIYA! HIYA!"

We immediately climbed another tower to scout out the next pizza slice. Eric grabbed it and covered us long enough to get to the next slice. We worked our way across the maze like that. By the time we got to our fourth slice of pizza, the ghosts were mad. Like, really mad. By now, they were flying around the maze at least twice as fast as we could run. We climbed on top of one more tower, and I mapped out a path to the breaker box. "I can make it!" I yelled to Eric. "You got the pizza?"

"Uh . . . "

No time to discuss. Ten pink fingers appeared next to Eric. We jumped off the tower, and I sprinted toward the box.

About halfway there, I realized I'd made a huge mistake.

The breaker box was way too far to reach in one run, and the orange ghost was catching up fast. "ERIC! WE COULD REALLY USE A PIZZA RIGHT NOW!"

BLOOP-BLOOP-BLOOP!

The orange ghost could smell blood. It seemed to speed up. I rounded the final corner and stumbled over a cord but didn't fall.

BLOOP-BLOOP-BLOOP!

The breaker box was about 15 feet away. That was 10 feet too far. I could feel the ghost behind me now—it felt like static electricity. In about five steps, it'd all be over. Time started to move in slow motion.

BLOOP!

I sucked in a sharp breath and tensed up.

BLOOP!

Something slammed into a tower at the far end of the hallway.

BLOOP!

Eric.

BLOOP!

Our eyes met, and Eric instantly recognized that I was about to get swallowed by the ghost.

BLOOP!

Without hesitating, Eric used all his might to push off the computer tower.

BLOOP!

I had a moment of confusion, then started screaming when I saw the red ghost round the corner behind Eric.

BLOOP!

Eric launched himself directly into the belly of the ghost.

CHAPTER 20
Emergency Exit

"AHHHHHH!"

Eric started screaming the most ear-piercing scream I'd ever heard. With the scream, the orange ghost behind me stopped in its tracks.

"ERIC!"

Eric's face froze, even as he continued screaming. His body turned gray and developed jagged cracks, just like the suit on the dinosaur planet. Then, his scream reached higher and higher pitches until it sounded digitized—like one of those auto-tuned songs.

"AHHHHHH!"

I sprinted toward Eric with tears streaming down my face. What was I supposed to do? Tear him away from the ghost? His arm would break off. I looked away. That's when I noticed the breaker box.

Of course.

It was probably too late, but I skidded to a stop anyway, threw open the metal door, and flipped every switch to "OFF."

The yellow lights immediately turned off. The computer hum went away too. Even the ghosts disappeared. The only thing that remained was the sound of Eric's scream. And that eventually faded too.

"AHHHHHHhhhhh . . . "

After a moment of silence, I called out, "Eric?"

No answer. I crept forward, my eyes adjusting to the dim red glow from an emergency exit sign. "Eric? Come on, buddy."

I stopped walking and listened. I heard ragged breathing.

"Eric! Talk to me!" When I reached my friend, I gasped. Yes, he was still alive, but he looked like he shouldn't be. Every inch of his body trembled. He had his hands balled into fists and his eyes squeezed shut.

I grabbed one of Eric's fists. "Eric, it's OK. They're gone. They're all gone."

"It . . . hurts."

"What hurts? Tell me what hurts."

"Hhhhhhhead."

"OK, I'll . . . " I stopped when I looked at Eric's head. I don't know exactly how to explain this, but his head looked like one of those clay projects you do in art class after it's been baked in the kiln. It was all lumpy with a bunch of hairline cracks. I gulped. "We'll get you bandaged up, OK?"

"Ch-ch-ch-ch . . . " Eric's teeth were chattering, but he finally got it out. "Chest."

"Your chest hurts too? That's no problem. We'll . . . "

Suddenly, Eric's eyes popped wide open. "FIRE! IT'S ON FIRE!" He started beating his chest.

"Stop! There's no fire!"

Eric wouldn't listen to me. He kept whacking his chest harder and harder until something cracked. Eric started moaning. "Ohhhhhhhhhhhhhhhhh."

My tears dripped onto Eric's body. "Just lie still, OK, buddy? I need you to lie still for me."

I looked up to collect my thoughts and noticed a security camera pointed at me. "Hey!" I yelled. "Hey! We solved your challenge!"

Nothing happened.

"You have to let us out!"

The camera continued to stare.

I stood up, snapped a knob off the nearest computer, marched to the camera, then threw the knob so hard my elbow hurt.

"YOU HAVE TO FIX HIM! DO YOU HEAR ME?! YOU HAVE TO!"

I was prying off another knob when I heard a click. I looked toward the noise and saw the door underneath the emergency exit sign creak open.

"Wait here!" I called to Eric as I marched toward the door. My body was overflowing with so much rage and adrenaline that I felt like I could punch through a wall.

"I'M HERE!" I yelled as I strode through the door.

Click. Click. Click.

Overhead lights flickered on to reveal a large office, empty except for a treasure chest, an oversize desk that held a laptop, and two figures—Max and the Hindenburg.

Max smiled. "Welcome, warrior."

CHAPTER 21

Supreme Ultimate Warrior

I ripped a page from Eric's playbook by marching up to Max, winding up, and punching as hard as I could. Just before I connected with his stomach, Max grabbed my fist.

He was finally real.

"That's not very nice."

"Fix him," I growled through clenched teeth.

Max *tsk-tsk-tsk*ed. "You made this much harder than it needed to be."

"We figured out *Pizza Boy*! Now you have to fix Eric!"

"What did you figure out exactly?"

"The breaker box! We shut down the whole thing."

"Oh, you thought you did that? Noooooooo. No, no, no. You didn't shut down anything."

"Yes, we did. All the lights turned off. The ghosts disappeared."

Max patted my head like I was a toddler. "That box doesn't do anything. My world doesn't need electricity to work. All it needs is my permission. See?" Max snapped his fingers, and the orange ghost reappeared 10 feet away and started charging. I didn't scream or flinch. Max waited until the ghost got an inch from my nose and snapped again. The ghost disappeared. "I shut off the game so we could have this little chat." Max leaned in a little. "See, I control everything here."

"Not the temperature," I shot back.

"Excuse me?"

I pointed to the sweat stains forming under Max's armpits. "The Reubenverse is overheating, isn't it? That's why everything's so hot."

"You're hot?" Max asked. "Why didn't you say so?" Suddenly, the room felt 20 degrees cooler. "Is that cold enough?" Everything turned to ice. "I can make it colder if you like." I tried to remain still, but I couldn't stop myself from shivering. Max snapped his fingers again, and the ceiling folded back on itself to reveal a raging blizzard. Wind whipped around the room, and snow started piling in the corners.

I shivered uncontrollably, and my fingers turned blue. I tried my hardest not to give Max the reaction he was looking for, but I finally gave up. "STOP!"

Max shrugged and snapped. Everything went back to normal. "If you start getting uncomfortable again, please let me know."

"Unnnnnnnnnng."

I spun around to see Eric shakily crawl into the room. In full light, he looked 10 times worse. Once he made it all the way inside, he collapsed and moaned again. "Unnnnnnnnnng."

"Oh my," Max said. "Is he well? He doesn't look well."

The sight of my best friend reenergized me. I wound up to punch again. This time, Max simply held up his hand, and I couldn't budge.

"Don't. Do. That," Max said. Then, he put down his hand, and my fist fell to my side.

Eric tried to stand, but something cracked, and he fell back down. "Unnnnnnnnnng."

"Shhh, shhh, shhh, just relax," Max said. He walked over to Eric and circled him twice. Then he looked at me. "You really did a number on your friend, didn't you?"

"You did this!"

"No, I didn't. I told you how to do this nicely. Remember? This is on you." Max touched Eric's head, and a bunch of hair came off in his hand.

My adrenaline went away, and I felt like collapsing. "Just make him better. Please. That's all I ask. Make him better and we'll never bother you again."

"You want to make things better? I'll give you a second chance." Max walked to his desk and pulled another glass of Dr Pepper from a drawer.

My breathing quickened when Max set down the soda on the desk—right next to his computer. This was my opportunity. I played along. "So—so if I drink that, Eric goes back to normal?"

"Oh, no no no. He'll never go back to normal," Max said. "Our actions have consequences. No, this will kill him. But it'll do it without pain!"

"You can't! Please."

"Listen. This is the hardest lesson you'll ever learn. But once you learn it, it'll change your life. You'll become a warrior." When I didn't move, Max changed tactics. "Look at him, Jesse. He's in pain. Drink and all that pain goes away. He wants you to do it."

I couldn't look at Eric anymore. "The pain will go away instantly?"

"The moment the first drop hits your tongue. I promise."

I breathed a deep sigh, then started walking toward the desk.

"That's it," Max said. "This is the moment you become a warrior."

I picked up the cup and looked down like I was trying to decide whether or not to drink it. My hand was even shaking, which was a nice touch.

"That's it," Max smiled. "Just one sip and it'll be over."

I lifted the cup to my mouth. Then, right at the last second, I flipped it and threw it at the computer.

I'd moved too fast for Max to stop me. The soda splashed all over the keyboard, and then the computer popped, fizzed, and hissed. I held my breath and looked at Max. He stared with his mouth open. Then his head started jerking. "Wha-wha-what did yoooooooooooou do?"

"I just saved the world!" I yelled.

"You aren't going to ge-ge-get away with . . . " Max froze.

I held my breath. What now? Had I destroyed the Reubenverse or just frozen it? I crept up to Max. He looked like a statue. I stared at him for a moment, then tapped his face.

"Pffffff!" Max wheezed, his mouth turning up into a grin.

I jumped back.

Max's wheeze turned into an all-out belly laugh that lasted an uncomfortably long time. "I'm sorry, I'm sorry. That was just really funny!" he said, wiping tears from his eyes. "So, to be clear, your big plan was spilling soda on my keyboard? And you thought, what, I'd explode or something? Here, let me try it again." Max started twitching his head with his eyes crossed. "Blub, blub, blub! I'm melting because some kid spilled pop on my computer! Hahaha!" Max slapped the Hindenburg on the back. The Hindenburg did not move, so it was unclear if he found this whole thing as funny as Max did.

I was dumbfounded. "I thought—isn't that the computer that controls everything?"

"You still don't get it, huh?" Max asked. "There is no master computer! That thing is whatever I say it is." Max pointed at the computer, and it turned into a banana. "You know why? *I'm* the computer!"

I felt sick and depressed. "What's next?" I mumbled.

"Oh, right! Well, I do have a prize for Ultimate Warriors." Max gestured to the treasure chest. "But I'm sorry to say that you failed the test and therefore are not Ultimate Warriors. So now I'll let the Hindenburg zap you two into a Black Box. Eric's going to writhe in pain for eternity, and you won't even be able to offer comfort because any time you touch him, he'll crumble like a granola bar." Max pretended to wipe a tear off his cheek. When he lifted his arm, he revealed that his armpit stain had spread down his shirt. He patted my head again, and I noticed that he smelled like body odor. "I want you to know that this isn't personal, and it's not happening because you're a bad kid. It's because you broke the rules of my world, and that means you're a bug. The Hindenburg's got to get rid of bugs. That's his job. You understand that, right?"

"Whatever," I said. "Put us in the Black Box. I don't care. But you've got to stop your Rapture thing. You can see the system's overheating, right?"

That snapped Max out of his cocky, condescending mood. "Nothing's overheating! It's fine!"

"It's not fine. Even you're sweating!"

Max turned red. "Everything is under control! Everything is under MY control!" He started pointing all over the room, causing trees to shoot up through the carpet, his desk to twist into a pretzel, and a waterfall to pour out of the left wall.

"Max . . . " I tried.

"IT'S 'SUPREME ULTIMATE WARRIOR!'" Max bellowed as he pointed to Eric, causing Eric's right hand to fall off.

Eric just stared at his missing hand in shock, too spent to even scream. Max strolled over to the hand, then casually kicked it. "Glitch," he said to the Hindenburg.

The Hindenburg immediately blasted the hand. It disappeared in a puff of smoke. All that was left was a burnt blue circle.

Max walked to me. "My world," he said coldly. "Everything I say is true. Everything."

Max stared at me like he needed to hear confirmation that I believed him, but I couldn't take my eyes off the burnt circle on the ground. I'd seen something like that before, hadn't I?

That's when I remembered. Beans.

That realization clicked everything into place for me. Suddenly, I saw Max for who he really was.

And that gave me an idea.

CHAPTER 22

The Glitch

"Could I look inside the treasure chest?" I blurted out.

The request took Max by surprise. "The what?"

"The treasure chest. I know we didn't win the challenge, but I really want to see what's inside before we go."

An evil grin spread across Max's face. "I'd love to show you." He pointed at the chest, and it creaked open.

I walked over and peeked inside. "It's empty."

Max chuckled. "People will come all this way for some treasure that's not even there! Isn't it funny?"

"It's what I expected."

Max waved me off. "No, it's not."

"Sure, it is! You had to have known certain people would start rising up against you, so you came up with this challenge to find them first. What warrior could resist a face-to-face meeting with the enemy? Then you made your challenge so impossible that it would kill anyone who tried it. This was never about the treasure. It was always a trap to kill your strongest competition before they could challenge your throne."

Max cocked an eyebrow, amused that I had figured it out. "It also let me have a little fun along the way."

"There's only one problem," I said. "That's not something an Ultimate Warrior would do."

Max shrugged. "That's your opinion."

"No, it's yours. Remember what you said? 'The Ultimate Warrior never backs down from a challenge.'"

"Whatever. Black Box time."

"But wait a second!" I was gaining steam. "You said you were not only an Ultimate Warrior. You claimed to be the *Supreme* Ultimate Warrior. So what's going on? Both things can't be true. That's called a . . . "

"Glitch!" Max interrupted and pointed at me. "He's a glitch!"

The Hindenburg stared at me with its blaster outstretched, unsure of what to do.

I smiled. "Remember Beans?"

"I said he's a glitch!" Max repeated to the Hindenburg.

"Beans was Eric's name for your courage challenge kitten. Beans broke the rules, didn't he? He clawed through the wall to save us." I pointed to the burnt blue circle where Eric's hand had been. "Beans got blasted by a Hindenburg because he did something he wasn't programmed to do."

By now, Max was redder than I'd ever seen him. He pointed at me, but the Hindenburg jumped between us. A ripple of energy bounced off the Hindenburg and caused Max to stumble backward.

"Once the Hindenburg showed up, you got the error report, just like you'd requested," I continued.

"STOP TALKING!"

"So you checked it out and panicked. Where did these two kids come from, and how could they have already beaten half your challenges?"

Max pointed at the ceiling, which crumbled over my head. The Hindenburg held up its fist, and a blue shield protected me from the rubble.

"In your panic, you started The Reuben Rapture early. That's why our watches still showed time left. You didn't have enough endurance to stick to the plan."

Max pointed at the floor, which disappeared under my feet. The Hindenburg grabbed me before I could fall.

"YOU!" Max pointed at the Hindenburg. "YOU'RE FIRED!"

"You can't fire Hindenburgs," I said. "They protect the rules and get rid of bugs. What if a bug started trying to delete a Hindenburg?"

Max was furious. He pressed a few buttons on his watch. "I'll figure this out." His face started to get pixel-y. Suddenly, the Hindenburg grabbed Max's neck, and he turned back to normal.

"You claimed to be the Supreme Ultimate Warrior, then you told us what that means," I said. "A warrior is someone who's strong and courageous. Someone who endures to the end. Someone who's wise. This is your world, and those are your words. They must be true. But they're not. How could they be? Today you proved that you're no stronger than a kitten. You're not courageous enough to face a fair challenge.

You're not willing to endure to the end. And you know what? It probably wasn't wise to let us stick around."

The Hindenburg held Max by the throat and stared at him through my whole speech.

"Do you want to see a warrior?" I pointed to Eric with a shaky finger. "There's a warrior."

The Hindenburg tightened its grip.

"You're no warrior, Max. You're a fake. You're a liar. And that makes you a glitch."

After I finished, I held my breath and watched the Hindenburg carefully. The alien stared down Max for five more seconds, then set him on the ground.

"Thank you." Max dusted himself off. "I'll be sure to . . . "

He stopped talking when he looked up to see the Hindenburg waving.

Bye-bye.

BLAST!

Just like that, Max was gone. But the Hindenburg wasn't done. After it finished blasting Max, it turned to Eric and waved.

"Wait!" I yelled.

BLAST!

I heard the blast but didn't see it. That's because a blinding white light rolled into the room just before the shot.

"ERIC!" I screamed, covering my eyes. I squinted and peeked between my fingers to find my friend. Instead, I saw the Hindenburg waving at me. He lifted his blaster, but the light swallowed him before he could shoot.

Then, the light swallowed me too.

WHOOSH!

NOW LOADING SERVERS ...

CHAPTER 23

Countdown

"WHO'S THAT?!"

I opened my eyes to see a gun poking in my face.

"Stand down!" someone else yelled. "It's a kid!"

I tried to look around, but the room was too dark to see much. All I could make out were the outlines of 20 or 30 gun-toting muscle men.

Another voice spoke up. "The temperature has stabilized! Bring back the power!" I recognized that voice! It was Mr. Gregory!

Lights clicked on all over the room, revealing that I'd beamed back into the computer tower room of Max's real-life San Francisco office. The room was filled with men in FBI vests. One of them escorted me to Mr. Gregory. "Excuse me, do you know who this is?"

"Not now, this is very . . . " Mr. Gregory glanced at me, then his eyes got wide. "Jesse?!"

"Where's Eric?" I asked.

"I don't . . . where did you . . . how could . . . " Mr. Gregory had a million questions, and his brain couldn't figure out which one to ask. Finally, he finished a sentence. "Did you do this?" he asked, pointing to a computer screen.

I took a closer look. The screen displayed a number that was quickly going down.

1,643,221. 994,576. 521,877.

"What's that?"

"The Reubenverse population!" Mr. Gregory said.

"Did—did we shut it down?"

"You tell me!"

I scrunched up my face and repeated my question. "Where's Eric?"

"We'll get to zero soon," Mr. Gregory said. "I imagine he'll be here any second."

133,592. 99,555. 77,628.

I started to panic. "No, he was doing bad in there! Really, really bad! We have to go back and save him!" Before anyone could stop me, I ran to the big

Reubenverse door and threw it open. There was no more swirling light—just a plain office wall.

One of the FBI guys put his hand on my shoulder. "Come on. We have to get you checked out."

"I'll go when Eric gets here!" I spun away and ran back to the tower.

23,003. 15,909. 11,777.

"You said he was in bad shape. What does that mean?" Mr. Gregory asked softly.

"He'd turned black and white, and his skin was getting all these cracks, and he kept breaking, and his hand—his hand . . . " I stopped talking and stared at the countdown so Mr. Gregory wouldn't see me cry.

Mr. Gregory put his hand on my back. "It's OK. It's gonna be OK."

I tried to believe him. Mr. Gregory knew a lot. He wouldn't tell me that Eric was going to be OK if he wasn't, right? But he hadn't been there—hadn't heard Eric's chest crack. A chest should never crack. When I replayed that sound in my mind, my head started hurting, my breathing got funny, and it became harder to hold the tears in. I stared at the countdown clock to keep my mind on track.

6,421. 4,453. 2,976.

Instead of imagining the worst, I tried to picture the movie version of this story. The room would be filled with silent tension, and the camera would focus on an FBI agent mouthing silent prayers. We'd wait and wait until the countdown got all the way down to 1. Just when all hope would seem to be lost, we'd hear a voice from the back of the room. "Miss me?" We'd all spin around at once to see Eric waving. Then everyone would cheer, happy music would play, and the camera would slowly pull back as we'd mob Eric.

I kept that happy image in my mind while the real-life countdown ticked lower and lower. It got all the way down to movie range.

5. 3. 1.

That last number lingered on the screen for a while. Then 0.

Eric never showed.

CHAPTER 24

Hulkamania

"Sounds like your friend was a real hero," an FBI agent said as we walked out of Max's headquarters that evening.

"Is," I corrected. "He is a hero. He's coming back."

The agent looked uncomfortable. "We checked all the servers. I'm sorry, but nobody else is in there."

"We'll see," I replied.

I would repeat that phrase a lot over the next several weeks . . . When a military nurse squeezed my hand while wheeling me inside a brain-scanning machine. "I'm sorry about your loss."

"We'll see."

. . . When an NSA agent looked up from his notes during one of our interviews. "Your buddy made a great sacrifice."

"We'll see."

. . . When a government psychiatrist started his spiel. "Losing a best friend . . . "

"We'll see."

The worst part came when people stopped feeling like they had to say something. They'd just look at me with sad eyes, taking away my opportunity to tell them that Eric would be OK. No matter how much time passed, I kept holding on to hope that Eric would return. He had to. Mr. Gregory said he would.

I'd tried again and again to talk to Mr. Gregory after my return, but I never got a chance. So many people blamed him for the Reubenverse disaster that the FBI had to put his whole family into hiding. I spread the message to all who would listen that this wasn't Mr. Gregory's fault—that he'd actually tried to stop Max. But almost everyone had a friend or family member who'd gotten sucked into the Reubenverse during Max's Rapture, and they had to hold someone responsible for their loved one's brief stay on Planet Peeved Porcupines. Sure, no one had died, but this was traumatic stuff. Since Max Reuben never returned, Mr. Gregory became the natural target for outrage.

But after a month or two, the outrage moved on to other issues, the government agents with fake smiles stopped showing up at my door, and newspeople quit calling for interviews. Things slowly returned to normal. The new normal. Without my best friend.

I tried to keep Eric's memory alive by talking about our adventures. Unfortunately, very few people could sit through an Eric story. Any time I tried bringing up our adventures with my mom, for example, she'd nod and follow along until I'd get to a sentence like, "The knifebots sliced at my face, but I rolled away." Then she'd get all panicky, and I'd finally mumble, "Never mind."

When school started back up, I began hanging out with Mark Whitman. Mark didn't talk a lot, but at least he understood what I'd been through. He'd patiently answer my questions about the Black Box even though I could tell he didn't like talking about it. I also started video-chatting with Sam from Australia. Although I remembered Sam being tough from our adventure together, she turned out to be an excellent listener. She let me talk and talk, and then she would pretend that the video quality was bad when I started tearing up so I wouldn't have to admit that I was crying.

Some days, I found it harder to maintain hope than others. Maybe the hardest day was the late-September Saturday when I picked up my stuff from Eric's house. I'd been over to Eric's house several times that summer when I'd remembered something I'd left in his basement. Each time I'd stop by, I could see that my presence was reopening a wound for Mrs. Conrad. Finally, I suggested a cleanup day when I could collect all my stuff at once.

That was a bigger job than I'd thought. The government agencies had long ago removed everything video game related, but I'd underestimated the mountain of junk Eric and I had accumulated. There was the bag of paper towel tubes, pinwheels, and yarn we'd collected in hopes of building the world's biggest marble track. There was the board game tub with pieces from all the games hopelessly mixed together. And then there was the closet filled with toy layers that archaeologists could use to date eras in the life of a child. There was the Mickey Mouse era, then the Bob the Builder era, then the Hot Wheels era, then the Teenage Mutant Ninja Turtles era. For much of the day, I quietly picked through the junk with Eric's parents.

Mr. Conrad pulled a bacon-shaped pillow out from behind the couch. "Yours?" he asked.

"Nope."

Mr. Conrad smelled the pillow, then wrinkled his nose and held it over a trash bag.

Mrs. Conrad shook her head. "That was one of Eric's favorites." Then she turned to me and held up a wrestling figure missing its head. "Is this trash?"

"Can we keep that?" I asked. "Eric and I were going to put a Hulk head on it, but we never found his old Hulk. I still think that would be cool."

"Oh, I found the Hulk," Mr. Conrad said. He dug through a box and pulled out a plastic Incredible Hulk action figure. I popped the head off, then snapped it onto the wrestling figure's body. I smiled. It fit perfectly.

Ding-dong!

The doorbell rang. Mrs. Conrad sighed. "I can't. I just can't. Can you get that, dear?"

Mr. Conrad's head popped up from behind the couch. "Give me a second."

"I can do it," I said.

"Are you sure?" Mrs. Conrad asked. "Just tell them we can't come to the door right now."

"OK." I walked up the stairs with the wrestling figure in my hand and opened the door.

"HULKAMANIA!" Eric yelled.

I dropped the wrestling figure. No way. No. Way. I opened my mouth to say something but just couldn't. Finally, I did the only thing I could think of. I poked Eric to see if he was real. My finger squished into his belly.

Before I could do anything else dumb, Eric swallowed me in a huge hug. "I never thought I'd see you again!"

I grabbed Eric and looked him up and down. His color had returned! No more cracks! He even had both hands! "Where were you?!" I finally asked.

"I don't know. It was dark and empty, and I was there for a really, really long time. But then Mr. Gregory got me out!" He pointed to a car in the street driven by someone who looked like Mr. Gregory, except if someone had replaced Mr. Gregory's pointy hair with a mop. The driver's eyes got wide, and he shook his head.

"I mean, not Mr. Gregory," Eric said. "Uh, Mr. Bob or something."

I thought about Eric stuck in a Black Box and felt sick. "I'm sorry for not being there for you. I'm so, so sorry."

"No way!" Eric said. "You saved everyone! Plus, I had this little guy to keep me company. Do you think my parents will let me keep him?!"

I looked down and gasped. Staring back at me from between Eric's legs was a kitten with the world's biggest eyes.

"BEANS!"

CHAPTER 25

Game Over

This story has a horrible, sad ending. You should go back and read the beginning and middle, because honestly, those are the only parts that will bring you joy.

OK, did it work? Did we get rid of all the people who skipped to the end of the book? Good. Because this story could not have a happier ending.

Of course Eric's parents let him keep Beans. They were so excited to see him that they probably would have let him keep a pet jackal. Fortunately, Beans was way better than a jackal. He was cute, obviously. But he was also smart. Probably the smartest cat that's ever lived. Because Eric had spent all that time in the Black Box teaching Beans tricks, Beans could now do handstand push-ups, use his tail as a pogo stick, meow 15 different Christmas carols, and dance the Hokey Pokey.

Eric was different too. While Mark Whitman had emerged from the Black Box quieter and shakier, Eric was now somehow even more excited about life. On his first day back, he took us to an ice cream parlor, where he sampled all 31 flavors and declared each to be the best he'd ever tasted. He couldn't stop petting cats and dogs. Eric gave up his cave-like basement and started spending all his time outdoors. Sometimes, especially when it was sunny, he'd drag me to the park after breakfast and wouldn't let us go home until after dark.

It was during one of these sunny park days when I finally worked up the courage to ask Eric the question that had been bothering me since he disappeared. Beans had just run ahead to greet an elderly couple (yes, we were walking Beans. I told you he was a weird cat), when I mumbled, "So did it, like, hurt?"

"What?" Eric asked.

"Max said you'd be writhing in pain inside the Black Box. Is that what happened?"

"No!" Eric replied. "I was so crumbly when the Hindenburg shot me that my whole body just blew away."

That made me stop walking. "What?! Then why didn't you die?"

Eric shrugged. "It was the weirdest thing—I didn't have a body in there. I could talk to Beans, but I couldn't touch him. Mr. Gregory said that my brain was the only thing that got uploaded to the Black Box."

I thought about that for a second. "That must have been lonely."

"It was for a while. Really lonely. But I had Beans."

At that exact moment, Beans made a jogger's day by blowing her a kiss.

"Also, I found out that my mind was amazing at remembering things. Like, if I concentrated super hard, I could play an entire video game in my head."

"Oh, wow."

"It was pretty cool, but that's not what got me through." Eric turned to me. "You got me through."

I looked at my shoes.

"Every time I started feeling depressed or lonely or whatever, I replayed all the cool stuff we did. I probably watched that strength challenge a million times. And whenever I felt like giving up, I remembered that thing you said about me being a warrior."

"You are a warrior," I quickly said.

Eric nodded. "You are too."

I looked back at my shoes and allowed myself a little smile. Maybe I was.

About the Author

Dustin Brady

Dustin Brady lives in Cleveland, Ohio, with his wife, Deserae; dog, Nugget; and kids. He has spent a good chunk of his life getting crushed over and over in *Super Smash Bros.* by his brother Jesse and friend Eric. You can learn what he's working on next at dustinbradybooks.com and e-mail him at dustin@dustinbradybooks.com.

Jesse Brady

Jesse Brady is a professional illustrator and animator, who lives in Pensacola, Florida. His wife, April, is an awesome illustrator too! When he was a kid, Jesse loved drawing pictures of his favorite video games, and he spent lots of time crushing his brother Dustin in *Super Smash Bros.* over and over again. You can see some of Jesse's best work at jessebradyart.com, and you can e-mail him at jessebradyart@gmail.com.

MORE TO EXPLORE

The first thing you'll learn when you start coding is that finishing a program feels amazing—for about two seconds. That feeling ends as soon as you test the code and discover that it doesn't work. No matter how good you get at programming, your work will always have "bugs," or tiny mistakes that break the program.

Unfortunately, Hindenburgs that automatically hunt and destroy computer bugs don't actually exist (yet). That means it's up to programmers to debug their own code. Sometimes, hunting for bugs in code can feel frustrating, hopeless, and more than a little painful. It's not just hunting for a needle in a haystack; it's hunting for a needle in a needlestack.

But don't despair! With the right approach, debugging can be fun. Use this four-step process to transform yourself into a real-life Hindenburg and fix any bug.

1. HUNT

Programmers often "step through code" to hunt for bugs. They do this by running the program through a "debugger" that allows them to pause each line of code to make sure it's doing its job correctly. If you step through your own code, start at the beginning and stop when you reach an unexpected result. You've found your bug!

2. INVESTIGATE

Now it's time to put on your detective hat and start asking questions. How is this result different from what you expected? Are you able to reproduce it? What does the error message say? You're not trying to solve the problem yet; you're just looking for clues you can use to fix it.

3. FIX

Use the clues you've gathered to come up with a solution. Have you seen anything like this before? What worked in the past? Have you checked for typos? You could ask for help from a teacher or paste your error message into Google. Sometimes, the best way to learn is through trial and error.

4. REPEAT

You've debugged! Congratulations. Give yourself a pat on the back, relax, and run your shiny, new . . . WHY IS THE PROGRAM STILL BROKEN?! Unfortunately, there's never just one bug. And sometimes, your "fix" breaks something else in the code. Take a deep breath, maybe step away for a minute, and then keep hunting. You can do it!

Hone your debugging skills in the real world by building a Rube Goldberg machine. Rube Goldberg machines are chains of marbles, dominos, pulleys, levers, and household knickknacks all working together to perform a simple task. They're a little like computer code because they're fun to build and never, ever work on the first try.

Follow the blueprint on the next page for your first Rube Goldberg machine. We're not going to give you specific instructions, measurements, or even materials, because half the fun is figuring it out for yourself. Just make sure your machine has these four parts:

1. MARBLE RUN

Build a ramp and find something to roll down it. The ramp can be made out of paper towel tubes, Hot Wheels track, pipes, or even books. And don't sweat it if you don't have a marble. You might choose a Ping-Pong ball, water balloon, lemon, or Matchbox car instead.

2. GROWING DOMINOS

For your domino run, try using different materials that start small and get bigger. For example, a domino might hit a wood block that hits a video game case that hits a *Trapped in a Video Game* book that hits a *Harry Potter* book.

3. BALLOON POPPER

Build a teeter-totter with a pin fastened on one end. Position the teeter-totter in such a way that the final domino pushes the pin up.

4. ICE DROP

Put ice into a balloon before blowing it up, then position the balloon over the pin on the end of the teeter-totter. Finally, place a cup underneath the balloon. Get ready for an ice-cold drink!

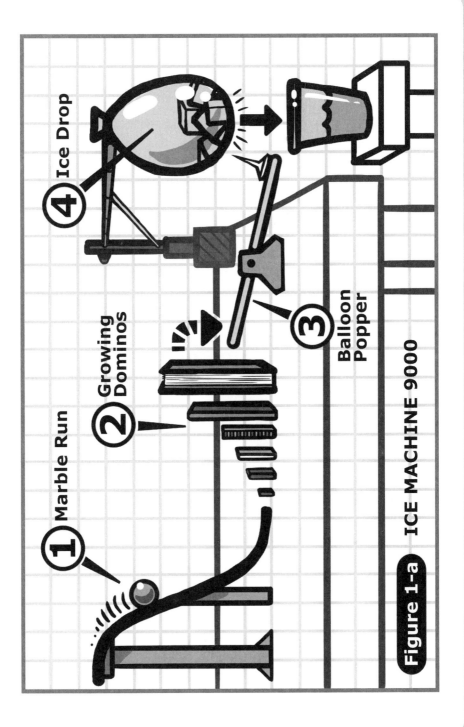

Figure 1-a ICE MACHINE 9000

Your ice machine probably won't work on the first try, and that's OK! Use our four-step debugging process to get things running smoothly. Start "stepping through" each section individually to pinpoint your problems. Run the section over and over until you completely understand the problem. Then, brainstorm solutions. You can try experimenting with the suggestions below. Repeat the process until the entire machine runs flawlessly.

1. MARBLE RUN

Problem: Marble flies off the tracks.

Possible solutions: Use enclosed tubing. Try a toy car with fixed wheels instead of a ball. Reduce the speed by shortening the run or giving it a more gradual slope.

Problem: Marble doesn't knock over the first domino.

Possible solutions: Make the ramp steeper. Use a heavier marble. Use guardrails to direct the marble.

2. GROWING DOMINOS

Problem: Dominos fall before they're ready.

Possible solutions: Work on a flat, level surface. Leave gaps throughout your chain until you're ready to start the machine so one fallen domino doesn't set off the whole run.

Problem: Some dominos don't fall.

Possible solutions: Find more dominos with in-between weights. Position the dominos farther apart so they hit each other with more force.

3. BALLOON POPPER

Problem: Pin won't pop the balloon.

Possible solutions: Use a heavier object for the last domino. Position the fulcrum closer to the domino so the pin hits the balloon with more force. Use a sharper pin.

Problem: Pin misses the balloon.

Possible solutions: Move the balloon closer to the pin. Fasten the teeter-totter board to the fulcrum that it rests on, so there's less random movement.

4. ICE DROP

Problem: Can't get ice into the balloon.

Possible solutions: Freeze ice into a tube shape instead of a standard cube. Partially fill the balloon with water first, then freeze it.

Problem: Ice won't fall into the cup.

Possible solutions: Position the balloon diagonally so the ice doesn't fall on top of the teeter-totter. Use more ice. Funnel the ice into the cup.

Look for these books!